New Earth
By: Hewson Duffy

Dedicated to the real Jordan who made me keep writing

ISBN: 978-1-304-69733-2

PROLOGUE

Liam James had been enjoying his day. After all, he didn't have to work because it was the ship's hundred and fifty-third anniversary, which invited a calm day of relaxing and watching television. It was 5:30 and the stars were out, as always, on the New Earth Search Ship (N.E.S.S.), which everyone called Nessie for short. Liam was watching an old Earth documentary about sharks when the picture of the jumping shark froze. Then the picture disappeared and a man's face replaced it. Confused, Liam looked outside his quarters to see if anybody else's screen had done it. All around there were heads of men and women who had obviously had the same thing happen. Even the announcement screen's normal red had been replaced by the man's face. Then the man started to talk. The booming voice of Edward Strand came through all the speakers.

"Hello fellow humans. My name is Edward Strand and I started the mission and funded the research that eventually made the ship around you. One hundred fifty years ago this day, your forefathers set out on this ship in a hope of finding life in the stars and a suitable planet if ours were to fail or run out of all natural resources. I am here to tell every one of you, that is a lie. This ship was sent out in hope of preserving the human race. In exactly one minute, a giant star will explode, or supernova, exploding with a force that will wipe out all life on Earth and make the solar system cease to exist. This ship will hold the last of the human race. The captain will now have stopped the ship, for it is well outside the blast radius. In a few months time the light from the supernova will reach your ship and it will be brighter than the others. Always remember you alone are the last of the human race and you decide its fate. Thank you." The broadcast ended and all the screens went back to normal.

Liam was still standing, open-mouthed, stunned at what he had just herd. There was a brief moment of silence, then chaos reigned. People were shouting questions at random, some were running around screaming, some people were frozen and open-mouthed looking like they had been hit by a heap of bricks. Children were crying for their mothers, there was the sound of breaking pottery, the ship's quarters were in a mess. A gunshot sound was heard and everyone stopped. One of the senior officers was standing in the hallway with a fake gun pointed at the ceiling.

"Everyone calm down!" He yelled. Everyone looked at his stern face. "Everybody just has to calm down. I know it's a harsh message, but would you rather be on Earth right now? We are the last of the human race, and there are fewer than 100,000 of us. What we don't need is people going crazy because our government lied to us. After all, it was for our own good. If people had known what this really was they would be paying all their money to get on it. This way it wasn't crazy from the start. What we need to do is just settle down and not start fighting. We will just have to know that there is no Earth for us to go back to."

He finished, and everyone seemed to calm down just a bit. There was no more yelling or screaming or chaos. Everyone went back to their homes and thought silently about the broadcast. Liam was one of the many people who didn't sleep that night.

Chapter One
20 Years later

My alarm woke me up with a deafening ring. After five seconds of covering my ears the sound stopped and I yawned. I had set the alarm to wake me up at six o'clock so I would have forty five minutes before having to catch the monorail to work. I got out of my tiny brown bed and rubbed my eyes. Almost without thought I walked into the next room, pressed three buttons and waited the five seconds before stepping into the small shower which had heated to 100 degrees for me.

After a short yet refreshing shower I got my work clothes on and walked into my kitchen, which was as small as all the other rooms in my living quarters. The kitchen had a medium-sized fridge, a microwave and a coffee maker on a counter in the corner. Per usual, I set the coffee maker to a mild brew with a little bit of milk and sugar. As the machine brewed, I pulled out a cereal box and a bowl out of a cabinet to the left of the fridge. The coffee machine dinged and I left my breakfast on the island while I got my coffee. I then sat down and eat and ate a hearty breakfast while thinking about work.

Twenty minutes later, I shut the door to my quarters and locked the door. I had gotten lucky with my quarters. I lived a mere three minutes away from the monorail station on foot, however on this day I was running late. The train that I usually took boarded at six forty five and left two minutes later. To make the train I would have to sprint, which would have been fine if I hadn't been wearing my work clothes. The uniform for H&D (Hewson & Duffy) offices was a simple button-down shirt with a tie, not exactly workout clothes however, I wasn't about to let my boss humiliate me again or give him a chance to yell at me. I sprinted as fast as I could, turning corners without thinking. I was dodging people left and right and within a minute I was at the monorail station where the doors of the monorail were still wide open. I stopped for a second to lean on a sign and catch my breath. I wouldn't be late, I thought to myself. I walked onto the train just as the doors closed, and fell down onto a seat.

The H&D offices were located in the center of the second ship. Nessie (N.E.S.S.) was not actually a full spaceship, but three big ships floating through space, connected by a single monorail. The ships were arranged straight across in a row. If you were to look at the ship from a bird's eye view the ship on the left would be the living quarters. This ship held rows upon rows of doors which lead to quarters just like my own, save for decorations which everyone was allowed to put up. Only families got bigger homes, and they were placed in a different section. The rules for getting a new home were simple: at sixteen, boys and girls were allowed to move out of their parent's home and pay for an unoccupied quarters, and if someone were to not like their home they would pay for a new one just like any sixteen year old might do. I was eighteen and had lived in my home comfortably for a year and a half. The second and main ship of Nessie was located in the middle of the three. It held all the shops, restaurants, clubs, small factories, courts, schools and even the cockpit in the front. This was where I spent most of my time. The third ship was probably the most useful, but the least used. Half of the ship was devoted to growing foods and animals for food and the other half to storage.

The jobs in the third ship were dreaded because they were really tiring, had long hours and only okay pay. It was an hour on the monorail to it and with an earlier start time than most jobs, an average worker would have to get up at five o'clock or earlier.

My job at the time should've been very nice. The telemarketing work was easy and the pay was good. However, the boss at the offices was not very likable and didn't like me. His name was Harry and from the first few days he had made it his job to make every single day at work my worst. He always found ways to humiliate me, make me miss fun events, and never get promoted. If I ever did anything wrong I knew I would be fired before anybody could say Nessie. I mean, didn't he have anything better to do than yell at me for doing my work? I had even once caught an online thief trying to hack our networks and Harry gave me a 10 credit bonus when I had saved him hundreds of thousands, maybe even millions. So, like any other day I wasn't looking forward to work.

At 7:05 I was sitting down at my desk waiting to hear the voice of Harry as he rushed in to send us our goals for the day. I always got the most boring which didn't take too long, but felt like it took hours longer than everybody else's job. While waiting I got on the screen and started trying to finish my program. When finished, the program that my friend from tech had helped me start would do my work for me, allowing me to chill the whole work time. However, making the program was hard and boring. I had been spending most of my time on it for the past month and I was almost done. I was working on it for a few minutes when I noticed what everyone else was noticing. Harry wasn't there. I had seen him a minute late once and it was only because of his power going out. It had been five minutes already without him showing up. Nobody wanted to call him or do anything of the sort for he was most likely going to be in a bad mood when he came and if you got in the way of Harry's bad moods he would find some reason to fire you.

Then at Seven-ten, the door opened. My breath slowed and I looked at my screen waiting for the voice I hated but knew would come. Instead, I heard someone with a very high voice, definitely not Harry's, say:

"Sorry I'm late everyone. Anyway I'm your new boss!" New boss, I thought. She might as well have announced that I had just won the lottery. I turned my chair around to see my new boss and standing there was a young lady dressed in a business suit. I knew that today work might not be so bad. I sat back in my chair feeling as if I was in heaven.

Chapter Two
New Earth

After my first good day at work, I exited the offices and I started to walk back towards the monorail. On a normal day, I would catch the 7:30 ride back to my home but something in me told me not to continue on to the monorail. After all, I had just had a great day at work so why not eat in this ship. I turned around and starting walking the opposite way. Though I didn't go into downtown very often, I knew my way around.

There were four main roads (there were no cars, just bikes and people, but we called them roads all the same) that made up downtown. One circled around the whole place and most factories and offices were placed around this loop, which was called Ocean Loop. The second road was called Europe and it led from the monorail station into every other road. The third street was named America and it wound through most of downtown, starting at Pearl and ending at the loop. The last street, Asia, went through the parts of downtown that America didn't and was rumored that if you worked on Asia Street you would have bad luck.

On this day I took Asia Street to see what restaurants I could find. The last time I had been down Asia Street was with my parents when I was only ten years old (since the ship was just drifting through space and there was no sun we just went by Earth time). I stared at the neon lights of the various shops as I walked. A couple minutes later I headed into a place called Arugula, which was an Italian pizza place. I ordered two slices of cheese and sat down at a booth.

Suddenly a buzzer sounded. I looked over to the table next to mine where a woman was sitting and covering her ears like she already knew the buzzer was going to sound. The noise stopped and I leaned over towards her and asked her if she knew what had just happened.

She gave me a weird look and said, "The broadcast is going to start soon. Duh." Realization dawned on me as she said it. How could I have forgotten, I thought. The yearly broadcast was today. Also, it was the twentieth anniversary of the original broadcast so it was bigger than normal. But, I thought to myself, it was pretty easy to forget. I mean sure it was really big, and it reminded us that we were the last of the human race, but when you have seen it fifteen times it just seems to drone on forever. I hadn't said anything to the woman but from the look on my face she seemed to understand. One of the cashiers called my name and I went up to get my pizza. I decided rather than to risk further embarrassment I would eat at my quarters. Also this way I would be out on the road when the broadcast was playing. Still, as I walked I could the voice of Edward Strand as he told the human race of the doomsday of Earth.

When I got on the monorail, the screen was just turning off, which was unusual because normally it would have ended ten minutes before I had gotten on. Not thinking too much about this I sat down and finished off my second piece of pizza. The monorail jerked and began accelerating.

Fifteen minutes later the doors of the monorail opened once again and I stepped off. Today was weekly movie night where my best friend Andreas and I would watch an old movie and I was looking forward to tonight's movie: The Matrix. Within a minute I was opening the door to my quarters where Andreas was already on the couch waiting for me.

"You're late" he said. I smiled. "I had a good day at work." I said and watched as Andreas gave me a look saying 'for real?'.

"Anyway," Andreas started with a meaningful look. "we're going into orbit." For the second time that day I was utterly confused and my face showed it.

"Going in orbit? Was that in the broadcast? Cause, I didn't see that." I said. Andreas burst out laughing.

"You miss everything don't you. Well you see in an extra message as part of the broadcast they announced that the ship will be going into orbit around a nearby star." He said in between laughs. I laughed and then sat down next to him on the couch. The television was already set up and Andreas pressed the play button on the remote.

Two hours later Andreas and I were talking about the end of the movie. It was action-packed, and still had held up a decent story. We were arguing about how it should have ended. I eventually won the argument (though he would claim otherwise) and he grabbed his sunglasses, his hat and his phone. He and I said goodbye and he left. I sat down on the couch and exhaled. So Nessie was going into orbit, I thought. We were becoming like another Earth. It was slightly funny. The lie that they had told everyone was that we were searching for new Earths and new life or resources. Now we were going in orbit around a star just like Earth did. Nessie gave life to all the human race just like Earth used to. We were becoming the exact thing that we were supposed to be looking for: a new Earth.

Snapping out of my musings, I got off the couch and headed into my bedroom and like many others I still was on autopilot thinking about the announcement. I felt like it shouldn't have been a big deal to me but I knew something would feel different when orbiting a star, like actually living on Earth.

Chapter Three
The Transmission

When I woke up the next day I was already happy. It was the weekend, which would normally mean shorter work hours. However, on this day I had the day off from work. I got one day off a month and today was the day. Sometimes I would get days off when Harry didn't want me there, which was fine by me, so I usually ended up with two or three days off a month. Since I was not working I had decided to sleep in. I had set my alarm for 8:00 rather than 6:00 so that I could sleep n peace. I hadn't planned much for this day except for it to be pretty lazy.

At 9:00 I was reading the announcements while riding the monorail towards the second ship. I had decided to try to explore the whole second ship; all the roads, all the businesses all the shops and everything else. When I got off the monorail I headed up Europe Avenue but instead of going on America or Asia I went on the loop and started looking at the various workplaces. After doing this for a few minutes I went back to one of the ones that had caught my eyes. It's name was Michael's Magic: magic supplies and kits, and had a picture of a magician showing the ace of diamonds. While walking towards it I noticed a very conspicuous alleyway in between Michael's magic and N.E.S.S. Realtors. Since I had nothing better to do I decided to investigate the alley after going into the magic shop.

The magic shop had a mysterious air to it and the lights were dimmed for effect. When I got to the counter the cashier spoke to me in a whispering voice. He told me how he could make Earth come back again and he produced from his clothes a crystal ball. He sat it down on the desk and it turned grey. Then he pulled the air above the ball up and to my surprise the ball started floating above the counter. I was astounded, and my jaw dropped. The magician smiled. He put his hands around the ball and closed his eyes as if trying to give his powers to the ball. When he opened his hands this time the ball had the image of Earth in it and was rotating slowly. I was so amazed I almost wanted to buy it, but then I saw the magnets underneath the counter top. The ball was magnetized and was floating because it was repelling the others. I smiled at the magician and looked down at thee magnets. I could see he knew what I meant and I walked to the door and left. I smiled, because I had beaten the magician's trick.

I then turned and went down the alleyway, which I noticed was unusually dark. Though, there was simulated sunlight all around this just made me more suspicious. I continued down the alleyway and I could notice it getting darker all around and when I looked behind it was lighter. It got so dark I could barely see the door right in front of me and crashed into it. I got up and felt around for the wall, and I felt a handle. Luckily for me the door was unlocked and when I opened it light flooded out into the alleyway. I was blinded for a second and couldn't see, but my eyes cleared up, and I saw a marble hallway with lights on the top. Without thinking I stepped into the hallway and the door slammed behind me.

I didn't know where I was or if I was allowed in this hallway, but the doorway was unlocked, so I convinced myself that I was allowed here. I was walking down the hallway, which was immaculate, for a minute or two and the hallway had not changed one bit. It still looked like the hallway went on infinitely, so I started to jog and then run.

After a few minutes of running I could finally see what looked like an ending to the hallway. I ran harder towards it but I realized it was only a turn. I stopped and walked around the turn and to my surprise I saw a door only a few yards away. I walked over to it and yet again the door wasn't locked. If someone was trying to hide something in this place they had done a poor job. I stepped through the door leaving it slightly ajar. What I saw inside almost made me yell. There were three computer screens set up next to each other with one keyboard and mouse. On the left of the room there was a door that said cockpit on it.

I was in the control center of Nessie. The computer was already on when I got inside, which intrigued me. The computer had three programs already open: a program that monitored the ship's systems, and two other programs I didn't know or get. A sense of power washed over me. All thoughts of how this wasn't really legal escaped my mind. I could control all the ship's instruments, announcement boards, monorails, though right now the ship was on autopilot. I started to open one of the programs that could show the place we were in and our route. However as soon as it started to run a password bar popped up and I closed the tab. I tried all the other special uses of the computer but all were password protected. I might have been able to access one of the things if I had finished the computer class in 10th grade but I had gotten kicked out for hacking. It then occurred to me that I could most likely hack some of the systems with some of my old techniques. I hesitated; I could get into pretty big trouble if someone found out I had hacked the control center, but then pushed the thought away and got to work.

Within ten minutes I had hacked into one of the first programs I had tried, by way of a formula I had worked out to hack cryptography. The program just controlled the radio transmitter on our ship which had been useful when we were traveling, for it could send out radio waves to see if they bounced off any big asteroids that could threaten the ship. The program had obviously not been used for many years though, because it was very slow to start up. However when it did it looked fairly new. I tried out some of its features and sent out a radio wave. Then I got it prepared to catch the radio wave if it bounced back.

As soon as I got this function running the machine started to beep loudly. It had a gotten a transmission but not the one I had sent out. I almost fell out of my chair. It was a signal from coordinates that every kid learned about in grade school. The signal was from Earth.

Chapter Four
Hope

My hands were shaking as I quickly turned down the volume. I silently hoped that no one had heard the beeps. I counted ten seconds, then let my breath out. No sooner than I did that, the door to the cockpit flew open and a young woman who looked about my age busted out of it. She looked livid and I thought I saw my life flashing before my eyes. However, when she saw me at the computer she looked confused.

"Who are you, and what are you doing in the control center?" She asked. I stuttered then gave a quick answer.

"That doesn't matter," I started, but she cut me off.

"This is completely illegal! You could be put in jail for this! Of course it matters!" She almost screamed.

"That doesn't compare to what I have found." I said in a slightly louder voice.

"Look!" I said even louder. She raised her eyebrows and I showed her the screen. Her face quickly turned from anger to surprise to disbelief then back to anger.

"These functions are password protected with layers of crypto. How did you get in?" She scowled. I almost yelled.

"I just found a signal from Earth, a Planet that should have been dead for the past twenty years, and your worrying about how I got on to this? We could've just made the biggest discovery since they discovered how to go as fast as light!" I said. She scowled but didn't scold me again. She seemed to calm herself then started to speak again.

"Okay then. So why don't we go and tell the actual people who run the control center about what we've found," she said, still seeming to be processing the information. I hesitated.

"What will we say? I asked. "We can't just walk in and be like hey I hacked into your computers and found this signal." I finished. She thought for a second, then slowly replied.

"I'll just say that we just saw it pop up on the screen as we were leaving and you investigated. Don't think I'm lying for you because I'm not! I could get in big trouble too for this." I had almost thought she was lying for me, but I capped the thought. I motioned for us to leave and we started back down the hallway.

Lots of looking around later we were standing behind the head of the control center who sat facing a N.E.S.S. meeting room. While walking to him we had gone over what we were going to say if more questions were asked. She would be the talker mostly but I knew the story so that if anyone asked me questions I could answer correctly. We had gone over tons of scenarios, which I thought was kind of dumb, but I didn't want to make her mad again. Among other things I told her my name was Jordan and she told me her name was Hope.

Hope took a deep breath and tapped the man on the shoulder. He spun around looking livid but then he saw who had tapped him and his anger seemed to subside. He was a bald man who looked about 70 years old, so we must have looked like kids to him. He was wearing a suit and tie and looked like a soldier that was scarred from battle.

"Yes." He said calmly. Hope took another deep breath and then started.

"Well sir, I was working in cockpit doing routine checks and I needed help with one of the new systems, so I got my friend Jordan here to help me. We finished our work, and were heading back through the control center when Jordan noticed a beeping noise coming from the computer and he went to investigate and he saw something that shouldn't be there." She paused.

"What did you see, boy?" The question was directed at me which I hadn't expected, but it wasn't that big a deal.

"I saw a that a radio wave had been intercepted. When I looked at where it came from it said the coordinates of..." I paused to increase the effect. “The coordinates of Earth, sir. I saw a transmission from Earth." The man's eyes were wide and his mouth was open but he quickly made his face impassive.

"Show me this transmission." He said, trying to sound skeptical but instead sounding like a little boy going to see a new toy. We smiled and beckoned him towards the loop and the alleyway.

<>

I was so lost in thought about how Earth could still be alive that I didn't even notice when we got to the door of the control center. We had left the computer on and the alert of the transmission coming in was still going in. He sat down in the chair and starting typing rapidly and a lot of text started flashing by. I couldn't tell for sure, but I thought he was checking the validity of the transmission. After a few minutes of silence and the text scrolling by, he sat back in his chair and blinked. At first he couldn't seem to find words but then started to speak in his calm tone.

"It seems you two have made a very important discovery. This could have just been one of Earth's old alien life form signals that has been bouncing around for years, but there is a chance that this was in the past 20 years. That would mean that somehow the supernova didn't hit Earth or there was no supernova at all. With the latest tech we could be back to Earth's coordinates in a couple months time. The council can't ignore this." The council was Nessie's government. It would have to vote on whether or not to fly back. The voting itself would take two weeks or so. I sighed. Still, there was a chance, however small that Earth was still alive. Nessie might finally touch Earth.

Chapter Five
Preparation

I sat down on my couch, staring yet not looking at the TV. The head of the control center had told Hope and me that he would have the decision ready for the council by the next day and they would vote in the next week. The thing he didn't mention, but all of us knew, was that when the council started voting on it the decision would be revealed to the public. The news, which didn't always have much to report, would go crazy. The bad thing was, most people would think the transmission was a hoax or from over twenty years ago and had been bouncing around for that long.

There was not much evidence that this was real because no one could accept that Edward Strand had been wrong. After all, everyone had seen the supernova in pictures or had really seen it if they were over 27. The most logical presumption was that the transmission was from a while ago. It was just something in my gut told me that maybe Earth was still there. Maybe the supernova never hit them. Maybe Edward Strand just made the wrong calculations about the blast radius. However, maybe was as good as I could get. There was no hope. The more I thought about it, the less likely it felt. I went to bed that night feeling defeated, thinking there was no chance the council would approve the trip back to Earth.

Completely forgetting about work I turned my TV on and started watching the news. I knew that soon a live report would come about the decision that the council was making. The first was about one of the latest movements by DFF, the Democratic Freedom Fighters. They were a group of rebel activists who were always going against the council and believed that we should we be able to elect our own council members if not abolish the council completely. They staged small stage protests around town and had once even caused a riot on Asia street. Their efforts were not very strong and all they usually managed to do was get on the news. After hearing a small part of one of their latest demonstrations, I turned the TV off and laid back. It was then I realized that though I had lessened hours, I still had work that day. I grabbed my stuff and sprinted out the door of my home.

I was a forty-five minutes late to work, but since our new boss; Heather, had been late she said it was okay just this once. The work was harder which I noticed but didn't say anything about. People on the phone seemed to be very irate and mean.

<>

When I opened the door to my quarters at 4:00 the door was already unlocked. The crime rate here was very low and burglaries were very rare so I was confused about who would be at my house. Only my parents and Andreas had the key, and they would have called me before going into my house. I was slightly scared to see who had gotten in but instead of a burglar I found Hope sitting in my living room.

"What are you doing here, and how did you get in here? I almost screamed. She tensed for a second then looked towards me.

"Well," she smiled. "That doesn't matter." I almost laughed but I stopped myself. "We have to practice for interviews." So she's thought about the publicity too, I thought. I came in, put my stuff down and sat down next to her on the couch. She told me the story again and then we took turns being the reporter asking each other interview questions. We did this for a while, then got to talking. We got on the subject of the previous day. She asked me how I had somehow gotten into the cockpit and I recounted the story. She stopped me after I had almost finished it.

"So you went into an unnaturally dark alleyway with a concealed door and just because it was unlocked you thought you could go into it without getting in trouble?" She laughed. "How can you know how to hack through the failsafe of a control system, but you couldn't figure out that maybe you weren't supposed to go through the door in the alleyway." She was cracking up. I laughed a bit too as I realized my stupidity. Hope started breathing normally again and got up.

"Well I better go, I have to eat dinner and it's getting late. See you later." She opened the door to leave. I waved and she rushed out the door slamming it behind her by accident. I looked at the TV. The time was 6:00, which wasn't exactly dinnertime, but it meant that we had spent two hours chatting and interviewing. I laid my head back. I said the word snack, and a small folding table popped up in front of me. I got up and went into the kitchen where a bowl of pretzels had popped out of a cabinet. I took the bowl off its perch and set it down on the scarred folding table. I turned back towards the counter and saw a message pop up on the tablet that I kept on the counter. It was from an unknown number, but the message told who the sender was.

896-555-7890: the brief is finished and the decision will be told to the council and public tomorrow.

I sighed. Everything would start tomorrow. I texted him a short thank you for the notification then I sat down on the couch, trying to take my mind off the decision and what the next day hold for me.

Chapter Six
The Voting

I awoke to the sound of my phone ringing. I vaguely wondered why I hadn't been woken up by my alarm, but I didn't think too much about it. I told the phone to read the message. It was from the captain of the control center. It read: The Voting (and press) starts at 8:00. I looked at my alarm clock which told me that the time was 7:30. Work had already started, but it would be soon clear to all of them why I had skipped.

The next half an hour was a blur. I got up, got dressed and had breakfast, but it seemed as if someone else was doing everything and I was just watching as I did everything sped up.

At 7:59 I sat down in my living room and turned on my TV. I counted down from ten as the intro to the morning news report was played.

"Hello, everyone! I'm Barbara Santos and welcome to today's morning news report. Right now we have some breaking news in the form of a decision that is being voted on right now. Vanity Vale reports." I smiled, knowing that soon I would be called in for an interview.

"Thank you Barb. I'm standing here at the doors of the council where inside they are voting on an extremely big decision. Apparently a teenage boy and girl were doing unofficial maintenance checks on the cockpit, when they heard a loud beeping from the control room. They looked at the monitors and saw that a signal from Earth had been picked up. Yes, that's right, Earth. Back when we left Earth almost 200 years ago we would be in the way of Earth's radio signals, meant to be picked up by aliens. This signal could mean that somehow Earth is still out there, or this signal could have been bouncing around for 20 years or more and it was just that we happened to come across it. So tonight folks, in what will have been their fastest voting yet, the council will decide whether or not to use some of our new tech to fly back to where Earth was, or is. Back to you, Barbara."

The report went on to people giving their vote and saying why they wanted to vote that side. I was soon bored and went to my bedroom to get my phone. As I picked it up, a loud ringing came from the phone and I answered the call.

"Hey, it's me," I heard the excited voice of Andreas say.

"Who else would it be?" I replied sarcastically though I had been expecting a news center to call. "Of course I heard about the council's newest decision it's all over the news. I said before Andreas could say anymore.

"Why were you looking at the news though? You're supposed to be at work." He sneered. I almost slapped myself. I was supposed to be working, I thought. I stuttered then said, "Well, work isn't that hard you know." I replied. I could almost see the smile on Andreas' face. However, not wanting to tell him too much, I hung up.

Yet almost as soon as I hung up the phone began to ring again. This time it was an unknown number so I knew it had to be a news corp. I answered.

"Hello," I said tentatively.

"Yes, is this Jordan Thorne?" Said a gruff voice.

"Yes." I said slowly.

"Would you consider doing an interview for the TNN report at 9:15? The studio is right where the loop starts." He said, which was very vague because no one knew where the loop started or ended. I took a deep breath before answering.

"Okay, I'll be there at nine o'clock sharp," I ended. This would be my first out of possibly many interviews. I laid back on my bed and rested.

<>

I was off the monorail at 8:45 just in case I got lost. Dressed nicely, I headed out of the dirty station and on to the street that would take me to the loop. The street was quiet for a day that seemed so awfully loud to me. After a few minutes I got to the loop. I chose to go to the right, which turned out to be right for soon the TNN studios came into view. I knew that I would be early, but at least I didn't get there late, I thought. I was soon standing in front of the big doors of the studio, getting ready for my tv debut. I took a deep breath and knocked on the doors. A young woman soon came and opened the door.

"Are you Jordan Thorne?" She said, giving me a nice smile. I nodded and she gestured for me to come in.

The studio was bigger than it looked. All around there were people rushing to get to their spots. They had sets for their talk shows and their news programs. The set that I would be on was the one people were rushing to the most. The cameras were set up and I could almost see myself sitting right next to Donald Shriner, the newscaster. I started to walk towards the set and as I did a seated man noticed me and ran over to me. He told me that his name was Ben Lewis and he was the executive producer for the show. My eyes widened as I shook his hand and he said he was glad to have me on the show. He told me where to go and who to talk to, and I soon felt that the interview was going to be a breeze. What I didn't expect was the phone call. One of the managers at the set was checking everything, when he got a phone call. The longer the call went on the more his face seemed to radiate his surprise. When the call ended he looked like he couldn't speak.

"The interview is still on, but we have gotten word that the voting has ended early. The vote was practically unanimous. All except for one voted to stay where we are and ignore the signal," He said.

Chapter Seven
The interview

I was stunned. I had never even considered that the council would deny the trip. Sure, all of our common beliefs told us that this signal was from Earth before the supernova, and there was only a small chance that this actually was from a surviving Earth, one that hasn't been killed by the supernova, but there was a chance, however small, that Nessie would touch Earth again. Couldn't the dumb council consider the chance that Earth might still be out there? My disbelief quickly turned to anger, but I kept it closed up in a small part of my mind. I reminded myself that I would have a chance to prove my points in the interview. I started to form out what I would say in my mind.

Soon I was sitting in a chair next to Mr. Shriner and the cameras were set up, ready to go. Some one yelled: "We are live in 5, 4, 3, 2, 1," The intro music played and I mentally focused myself.

"Hello, everybody welcome to the TNN morning report. I'm Donald Shriner, Today we have an exclusive interview with Jordan Thorne, the man who saw the signal from Earth. Though the council has officially rejected the proposal to go back to the coordinates of Earth, Jordan can tell us his story and opinion. But before that here are some words from our sponsors."

The cameras shut off as it went to a commercial break. I exhaled. The commercial break was only three minutes, so already people were getting ready for us to go live again. I watched on a screen behind the cameras that was showing what a normal television would show. The ad was for a brand of energy drink called 'Red Cow', that was 'a proud sponsor of the TNN morning news report'. Someone shouted a warning of fifteen seconds till we were live again. I mentally prepared myself as there was another countdown.

"Welcome back! Here we have Jordan Thorne, who was one of the two to discover this signal from Earth. Jordan, can you recount for us what happened and what you saw?" The newsman looked at me. I nodded and began to recount the well-rehearsed story.

"Well, we're really just the ones who saw the signal being picked up, nothing more. I had gotten a call from my friend Hope."

(We had decided that it was necessary for us to be considered friends for the story to work.)

"She works maintenance in the cockpit and had found a faulty circuit. She called because she needed help fixing the circuit, so I came and helped and as we were leaving we noticed a beeping sound coming from the control center. The computer showed that a radio wave had been received and that it came from the coordinates of Earth. We then rushed out and found the man who actually runs the control center. He looked at it and then got someone to get a decision about going back towards Earth to the council. Then just now I heard from one of the producers that the voting had ended early. " I finished and there was silence for a second. Donald looked impressed.

"Well, could you tell us your opinion about the council's decision?" He asked. I was prepared for this and started with a short answer.

"I will respect what the council says, but I think they made the wrong decision," I said, not showing any expression on my face. I knew the answer wouldn't be enough for him.

"What do you mean by wrong?" he said.

"Well, though it is a small chance that Earth still exists somehow, maybe Earth was actually out of the blast and or radiation radius of the supernova. Maybe it wasn't, and this would be a waste of time, but if it isn't we might finally see trees again, we might be able to touch Earth again, we might feel rain again, we might, just might feel the sun again." I finished and again there was a moment of silence, this one longer.

"Those were some very philosophical words Jordan, you have moved me. Now to Sprightley with our other news of the morning." He stopped and the red light on the cameras turned off indicating that we weren't live anymore. I exhaled and ran my hands through my specially combed hair. It was done, and my message had been heard.

I shook hands with the producer and then went out the door into the loop. I turned my phone back on. There were two missed calls from an unknown number that had been missed a minute ago. I called the number back and it picked up on the first ring.

"What were you doing? You should have called me before going on the news!" I knew the exasperated tone and voice from the first word. It was Hope. She took a breath then continued scolding me.

"You should have asked before saying that stuff. We have to coordinate! Now our opinion is sealed and we can't change it!" she finished.

"You sound pretty sad about our opinion. I thought it was a good one, plus it was honest. And why can't you have your own opinion. Seriously though didn't you want the council to approve our proposal?" I replied. I could hear her stuttering for a second then she said, "Your opinion is fine. But that's not the point!" I interrupted her.

"I'm sorry, mom," I said, letting the word resonate. "I should've told you." I finished with a kid voice. I could almost see the look of anger on Hope's face. I imagined steam coming out of her ears and I laughed.

"What are you laughing abou-" She got cut off as I heard the bing of a text from her phone as well as mine. I hung up and looked at the text message. I couldn't believe my eyes. I looked again, but the message was still there.

It was a text from the control center manager. 'The council has decided to reconsider. We may have a good chance this time.'

Chapter Eight
DFF

It couldn't be true, I told myself, it couldn't! The council had never even reflected on previous decisions much less reconsidered them. Once the council made a decision that was that, and no one ever dared say that they should reconsider. This was completely against their rules. I was surprised they didn't have a vote to consider whether or not to reconsider. Yet still, this was good because it meant there was a chance that we would make the journey. Also, since the council had actually reconsidered the decision, it most likely meant that they were going to say yes to the decision this time around. I was elated. We might really go back to Earth, I thought. I picked up my phone and smiled. I pressed a button and it called the last caller. Hope picked up on the first ring. She jumped into conversation as soon she picked up.

"It's against the rules! The council is breaking their own rules. They can't reconsider! This is outra-" I held the phone away from my ear and when I couldn't hear yelling on the line I put the phone back to my ear.

"Are you saying that you aren't happy that the council is reconsidering?" I asked her incredulously. I could hear her fuming as usual.

"Did you even listen to what I said?" She asked.

"No," I replied, "why would I want to? I lost you at 'they're breaking their own rules'. Who cares anyway. If you haven't noticed we have broken a lot of rules to get here." I heard Hope try to say something a few times but in the end she just sighed.

"Whatever. Forget it." She said in a defeated tone. I smiled to myself, told her goodbye then hung up. I sighed too.

I spent the rest of the day traveling around town trying to find new appliances, buying replacements, working out, and grocery shopping. At the end of the day I went to a grill and had juicy ribs while watching the news. Not surprisingly the main story was the council deciding a decision and deciding to reconsider in the same hour. The story wasn't very interesting, however, because I already knew what they were saying. It wasn't very interesting, that is, until they mentioned the date for the results of the decision: the results of the reconsideration would be released the next day.

Everything was happening so fast. Normally the council would accept a decision then actually vote on it a week later. They must've given this decision priority over others or just hadn't had any other imminent decisions. Still, everything seemed to be happening in the course of a long day. I paid the bill and got up to leave. It was eleven o'clock, so I decided to go to bed. I walked back to the monorail station and sat down on one of the benches. The next monorail wouldn't come for fifteen minutes. I felt my eyes close, and soon I dozed off.

When I woke it all the street lights were off. The monorails doors were open, so I got up and rushed through the doors just as they closed. I looked at the other person aboard. He was a man who looked about thirty, with curly blonde hair coming out of a beanie. He was reading the paper but when I stepped in and the doors closed he looked up. He blinked, and looked confused for a second then his eyes widened.

"Are you Jordan Throne?" he asked, looking intrigued and disbelieving.

"Yes," I replied, looking at my shoes. "and it's Thorne, not throne." To have something to look at other than my feet, I pulled out my phone to check the time. I could hear him saying something but I wasn't paying attention. It was three o'clock. No wonder no one was on the monorail, I thought. I snapped out of my thought just in time to hear the man say: "You here at three o'clock In the morning." He finished. Not wanting to sound rude I pretended to have heard what he said and I replied.

"Why are you here at three in the morning?" The question was blunt, but it was meant to shut him up. However, he seemed to take this as a queue to keep talking.

"I had to work late at my shift." He said, sounding faint and by the look on his face I could tell he was lying. "So, as I was saying why are you up this late?" I didn't want to embarrass myself, or frankly to talk any longer.

"I have my reasons. You obviously have them too." I said in a way that told him I knew he was lying. This time he shut up.

When I got back home, I didn't bother doing much of anything except crashing onto my bed. I was really tired still, yet I couldn't fall asleep. I just lay there for what seemed like eternity. Hours passed, and it felt like I would have finally fallen asleep but my alarm rang. I was drenched in sweat and I was about to fall asleep, but I got up. I was so tired I forgot completely about my job and all I did was get out my laptop.

I didn't really know what I was doing, but I vaguely remember thinking about searching the web for information and to see if the council had said anything more on the decision. It was on the website for TNN that I noticed the video. It was on the front and had a big article on it. All tiredness forgotten, I clicked on the video that was by the DFF and had gone viral. The video was of a man I recognized as the leader of the DFF.

"This ship's council just broke all their rules. They made a clear statement on a decision completely denying it. For now let's not worry about the decision, but they made a clear decision and now they are questioning their own judgement. For all we know they might 'reconsider' their own laws. Are these really the people you want leading your ship? The people that can't even follow their own rules. And, don't even get me started on the proposed trip. It's expensive, dumb, inefficient, and overall a bad way to spend this ship's energy. I'm not going to try to persuade you to join us, the Democratic

Freedom Fighters, I'm just going to say this. In a democratic society the people would vote a decision as big as this. So what we are going to do is let you vote. Click on the link below and cast your vote on this decision. When the council unveils their new Decision we will tell them what the people think, not what the council thinks. Thank you."

I was frozen in place. I remember just before blacking out that this could stop the trip to Earth, or start protests against it. Then I laid back in my chair and fell asleep.

I didn't wake up until I felt the slap across my face.

Chapter Nine
The Democratic Voting

I opened my eyes and felt a searing pain in my cheek. For some reason I felt like my hair was wet. I looked up and saw Hope's smiling face.

"How the heck did you get into my home?" I said angrily. "And why'd you just slap me? What I did do?"

"I slapped you because you wouldn't wake up. I screamed, slammed the door, shined a light in your eyes, threw an apple at your chest, poured a bucket of water on your head, and then had the idea to slap you. At least it worked." She paused and seemed to be deciding whether to continue. "As for how I got into your room, that's classified.

Anyway, why haven't you woken up yet? It's one o'clock in the afternoon. Don't you have a job?" She sounded not exactly exasperated, but tired of me. I yawned.

"Don't you have a job? What're you doing here anyway? Never mind why I'm sleeping in, stop acting like you're my mom!" I yelled, then turned over onto my stomach. There was silence for a few moments and I thought she might be leaving and letting me sleep. However she started speaking again.

"Okay. So I came here because Bill, the control center guy, is getting kind of suspicious, and because the council will decide in," she checked her watch, "five minutes whether or not to take the trip back to Earth. And just to make things worse, the DFF is against the trip back, and wants to overthrow the council because they're breaking their own rules." She counted the reasons off on her hand.

"I saw the video, you know," I yawned. "The message was pretty dang good, they're bound to have some new followers just from that." I finished and yawned again.

"Yeah, their message of having the people vote for themselves was a real hit. The video already has over 36,000 views!" Whoa, I thought. Nessie had a population of about 46,000. That was more than three quarters of the whole ship and counting.

"Wow," I said in an astonished voice. "Well, what're you waiting for? Turn on my laptop. It's on the counter in the kitchen." Hope rushed out of my bedroom and I got up.

When Hope got back, computer in hand, I was dressed and sitting on the side of my bed. She brought the computer over to me and sat down. I looked and saw what she was looking at. The DFF was live. The DFF logo covered the screen. It stayed there for half a minute while Hope and I stared, waiting for something to happen as the stream queued up. Then suddenly the DFF logo cut to black screen and then into the live stream. The same man from the first video was talking, and he was in the middle of his speech.

"Time we will release the people's voting results and compare. Just think, will you be able to trust your council, your deciding government, if their answer is different than the general public's answer?" He paused, smiling. Hope and I were still glued to the man's face, our mouths open and eyes wide. Suddenly a timer counting down from a minute appeared on screen at the top right of the video. The DFF leader looked towards the timer then looked back.

"In less than a minute your very own council will make the decision, and we'll show the results of our poll." He said it all in a nonchalant way, yet sounded happy at the prospect of defying the council. He looked up at the timer again as if he could see it.

"Thirty seconds till the results." I was breathing heavily and sweating. It all came down to this, though I thought it was very obvious what was going to happen. The council would clear the decision and the poll would show that the people said otherwise. I closed my eyes and waited. It was only a little over thirty seconds, but to me it felt like thirty minutes before the talking resumed and I opened my eyes. The screen had cut to a shot of the council building and one of the oldest council members had just walked out to greet the press. He looked solemn as he began to talk.

"The council of N.E.S.S. has made the decision. It was very close but we have decided in favor of taking the trip back to where Earth was, or is. This decision is final." His words rang through the bedroom and seemed to echo in my ears. The video cut back to the DFF leader who had the trace of a smile on his face.

"Now to our correspondent with the results from our poll," he said, and the video cut to a man in a suit sitting at a desk, looking like he was a news reporter. The reporter stood up and walked around to the front of the desk.

"Yesterday we released a promotional video for our poll, and that was spread around enough by news centers and such, that 72% of the population voted. Lets see what the results are!" The tension in the room could almost be seen. A graph appeared on screen labeled: poll results. The first bar was colored green and showed the percentage of the people who had wanted the trip. The second was red and showed the percentage of people that hadn't wanted the council to say yes. I sighed and shook my head. The red bar held 73% of the votes, while the green bar held only 27% of the votes. The correspondent pointed to the bar graph. "It's all there. The majority of the population wants to veto this decision. So ask yourself, if the council does the exact opposite of what the people want then why re they deciding for us. These people and this government is so corrupt that they will break their own rules just to make the wrong decision. Think about that." He stopped and let his words sink in.

"Now, there is a way to stop this corruption in our government. It will only work, though, if we have all of you. We must unite to vanquish this evil, this chaos. Together we can make a new government that will be of the people. We can stop this trip and stop the council. Join the democratic freedom fighters today and help make a better N.E.S.S."

The live stream ended and I sat glued to the screen, replaying the video in my mind. They were trying to get more followers. The DFF was always trying to get followers, but this seemed to me like something bigger. The message was a lot bigger, and probably would gain lots more followers for the DFF, but what would they do then, rebel against the council? No, I thought, they would do something else probably, bigger riots and protests. I didn't know why but somehow, though the video should have been small to me, it seemed like a huge deal in my head. I cut off my musings though and got up.

"So, they're recruiting more followers," I said, looking at Hope. I hoped inside that she had some of the same feelings about the video as I did. I wanted to know if she knew or had theories on why they were recruiting.

"Yeah, and it seems like they're going to try to launch something against the council. A war would be hard, because there are only a couple of real guns in storage, if any, and you have to be a high ranking person to get to get your hands on one of them. Still, they sounded like they're recruiting for a rebellion, which would be crazy, especially if Earth wasn't there." She said in a puzzled voice. I nodded. I walked back into my kitchen and Hope followed me with the laptop under her arm.

"Just if Bill asks anything tell him our story again, and again. If people hear things enough, they will believe them." I said, referring back to the beginning of the conversation, hoping to get Hope out of my room so I could go back to sleep. She caught my drift, nodded and headed to my door. I rubbed my eyes while walking back into my bedroom and fell back on to my bed. I was asleep within minutes.

Chapter Ten
Mathers

After the excitement of the previous few days, everything seemed to move in a blur of boring. I felt like I was asleep the whole week. I did everything normally, but I was just tired all the time. The week was just sleeping, talking, working, and eating. In a broadcast, one of the pilots announced that they were currently turning around the ship around towards the coordinates of Earth. If Harry had still been my boss I would have gotten fired before someone could say Nessie. Since the events of the council and the signal from Earth everyone had agreed to keep me on the job, and Heather had never really been for my leaving. Yet, I had skipped work so Heather didn't give me my paycheck that week, which was harsh, but better than being laid off.

During the week, the news held more updates on the DFF's new campaign and such, Andreas and I had movie night and Hope mysteriously got inside into my house again to give updates which were not very new or interesting. A week after sitting in my bedroom watching the DFF live stream I was sitting in the same place on my bed, not very tired anymore but bored out of my mind. I inhaled deeply, and exhaled. I was out of work for the day and I already eaten Chinese takeout. I had been tired the whole week yet now I was wide awake. I thought I had been tired from the action but now all I wanted was more of it. I looked at the time. It was 9:45, so not very late at all. I got up and picked up my key. I didn't know what I was doing, so I decided to go to someone who probably didn't know what he was doing either.

Soon I was stepping out my door and heading along the hallway in the opposite direction of the monorail station. I turned left into the stairwell and started walking up the flight of stairs to level two. Once at level two I turned left out of the stairwell and into a long hallway. I jogged down it then turned right, left, right, and right again then stopped to catch my breath. I walked the rest of the hallway to the plain brown door. The door looked like every single other one in this hallway, but to me this door was a gateway to good times. The door to was to Andreas' home. I opened the door and found Andreas watching a movie called Epic. The movie was from the makers of The Matrix and was another action movie. He heard me come in and looked up.

"Bored?" He said looking back to the movie.

"Yeah, that's a good movie by the way," I answered, walking over to his couch. Andreas nodded.

"So... how are things going with your girlfriend?" He said, in a normal voice. I gave him a funny look.

"What girlfriend?" I asked. I didn't have a girlfriend. I didn't know what he was talking about.

"The one that came a week ago and was all like 'I'm a friend of Jordan's and I need the keys to his quarters and he has said you're his best friend so...'. Well I gave her the keys and she still hasn't returned them. Anyway you're telling me that you don't know this girl?" I was enraged.

"Hope. I know her. She was the girl that was with me when I saw the signal from Earth." I said, dawning a look of understanding on Andreas' face. "Anyway see you, I'm going to go talk to Hope. Do you know where she lives?" I asked.

"Third floor, second door after two rights. I'm pretty sure." He replied and without a backward glance at him I walked out the door.

A flight of stairs and two right turns later, I stood outside Hope's door and waited after knocking on the door loudly. I waited ten seconds, then thirty, then a minute. Then Hope finally came to the door.

"How did you find my home?" She asked. "Same way you did. Andreas."I said in an annoyed tone. "

"Oh him, cool. Well you're just in time because I just got something that I was going to call you about. Someone wants us for a job, I don't know who or what the job is but they left a message on my phone that said it was for us. Listen." She finished and pulled out her phone. She pressed the screen a couple times and the message played.

"Good afternoon. We are looking for people that have a..." The man paused. "Certain skill set and you and Mr. Thorne will fit perfectly. You will be paid very well and the job will be very interesting. If you are interested in helping us then please meet us at #46, America Street. Thank you." The message ended with a beep and I looked at Hope.

"I'll see you at America street tomorrow then. Bye." Then before she reply I was out her door and off. Tomorrow couldn't come fast enough, I thought.

12 hours later
****

I stood outside #46 America Street waiting for Hope to arrive. The door to the building was plain and didn't even have a sign saying what it held. It was one of the places you walked past and just never noticed. It looked somewhat like a maintenance door. I tapped my foot a few times. I had skipped work for this, so it had better be good, I thought. I looked around and spotted the figure of Hope walking towards me. Once she had gotten to me I turned around once again and opened the door for Hope. She stepped inside the place and so did I.

The door slammed behind us and echoed across the dimly lit hallway. I walked down it behind Hope, looking at our surroundings. The hallway had old dim lights in a string at the top that looked like they should be in an antiques shop. The walls had chipping green paint that looked just as old as the lights. There was a door at the end, but unlike the hallway, it looked completely modern. It was metal and looked immaculate. We reached the door and it opened easily. We then found ourselves inside what seemed like a high-tech office. There were only six cubicles, except the computers looked state of the art. There was a meeting room with touch pads at every seat. Holographic displays were popping up at worktables. There was a front desk, and an announcements board that looked 3D. I took the lead this time and walked up to the front desk.

"Hi, I'm Jordan Thorne here to see whoever left the shady message on Hope's phone." The woman looked up. She looked at me inquisitively then stretched her neck to see Hope behind me. She said nothing for a second and gave us a cold stare. Then, all coldness evaporating she smiled and started to talk.

"Ah, Mr. Mathers will see you now. Turn right then keep going straight. Eventually you'll get to his office." She looked back down at her papers like she couldn't care less about us anymore. I turned on my heels, and with Hope right behind me; I walked as directed to the office of Mr. Mathers.

When we got inside the office Mr. Mathers was waiting for us and already was standing up prepared to talk.

"So, Mr. Shady, would you mind telling us why we're here and why all the secrecy in the message. You told us nothing!" I said, trying to sound annoyed at him rather then intrigued. By the smile on on his face, though, I could tell he knew I wasn't really mad or annoyed.

"The message was kept to as little as we could tell you in case your phone," he pointed to Hope, "was tapped. No, we are not this ship's secret service, but we are something like it. We were the only ones to know of this ship's true purpose until it was revealed to the general public. Our founder was Edward Strand and our sole purpose then and now is to preserve the human race, and though our founder may have been wrong about the fate of Earth he may also have been right. So we can't take our chances believing in Earth until we see it. Now, if you're asking why we're bringing you into this and why is it important I can also answer those questions. As you might know, the DFF has launched a new recruiting campaign, which has been doing very well. As far as we know they're planning some sort of rebellion or war.

This is where we come in. We're gathering intel on the DFF because whenever this war happens we want to know at least what they're planning and how to stop them in a worst case scenario. In the best-case scenario, we hope to shut down the DFF before they go big. As to why you two have been brought into our trust circle, we want you for your expertise as well as the fact that you two are somewhat of a symbol. If the DFF had you on their side, you would be like a symbol because people already know who you are. So, any questions?" I raised my hand. He looked around the room as if trying to find other hands. I rolled my eyes and put my hand down.

"What expertise do we have? I mean, I don't know about Hope, but I'm not really an expert at anything, except for maybe getting my boss mad at me." I said, in a matter of fact way. He smiled.

"When I say your expertise I mean your abilities with computers," he said abilities in a way that made it obvious he meant hacking.

"And your story-telling skills. I thought it was a well rehearsed one you told to the press." He stopped, but seeing the looks of wonder on our faces he continued. "Oh, c'mon you really think Bill couldn't figure out that you hacked into his computers? He has been running those for over thirty years, of course he knew that the radio signal program couldn't have just been left on. So anyway, will you help us? You will be doing mostly fieldwork, except for a bit of online hacking from our ship hacker here. Your salary will be a lot higher, that I can guarantee. And I'm pretty sure it will be more eventful than maintenance and office work. So, do you accept?" He said, tilting his head and folding his hands.

Chapter Eleven
Decisions

"Yea-no." We both said a different answer. I looked at Hope with a weird look and saw the same look reflected back at me. Mathers saw this and quietly stepped out of the room. As soon as he was out we both started talking.

"We shouldn't do this!" I started, but Hope cut me off.

"It's the chance of a lifetime, plus I--" I cut her off.

"No, it sounds dangerous and we could die or get really hurt." Hope stopped trying to cut in and I hoped this had made an impact on her. Then she started up again.

"It may be slightly dangerous but where's the fun in not taking risk? As well, it's not like our day jobs will be as good as this," she said. I tried to make a comeback to her argument a few times but the words wouldn't come out.

"Fine. But if we die I get to say I told you so in heaven! I said jokingly. Hope laughed.

"Good luck with that," She said and opened the door saying, "we've decided," to the room outside. Mathers then walked back in and looked inquisitively at us.

"We will do it." Hope said and I nodded in consent. Mathews then ushered us out of his office and down the hallway, past the cubicles and turned into the meeting room.

"Here is the meeting, briefing, and debriefing room. You'll meet me here tomorrow for your first assignment. This room is equipped with touch pads at every seat to show assignments and new intel. You'll be coming here a lot in between assignments, which may be as much as a month, but may be as little as a couple of days. You two will be partners for assignments mostly, though sometimes you will be joined by others in bigger assignments. So, tomorrow both of you'll get the official tour of this place and get your first assignment. The tour starts at 9:30 so don't be late. Oh, and I almost forgot your salary will start at 50 credits an hour but depending on how well you use your time and finish assignments you could be making up to 150 credits an hour." He paused and seemed to be trying to remember something else. He almost said something but then stopped. The second time he started the words came out. "That is all. You may leave now," he said and ushered us out of the room.

On our way out of the offices I looked at the cubicles and at the people in and around them. The people who were standing up were rushing around handing files and such to those sitting down. The ones sitting down were completely focused on the screens in front of them and every so often without looking up one of them would shout a file name or something they needed to be given or needed to download. I noticed that there weren't actually that many people in the offices, but I figured this was because the assignments were mostly in the field. As we walked back down the antique hallway I pulled my phone out of my pocket and I checked the time. It was 12:13, a little more then an hour since I had been waiting out here for Hope to arrive.

We got outside once more and I looked to the right of me at Hope. She didn't look back and instead started towards the monorail station. I followed. As we walked back to the station I tried to even my pace with hers but when I got closer to her she would walk faster. I tried to walk next to her again but she greatened her pace even more. I almost started to jog to catch up with her the third time, and this time she started running away. I gave up and started walking normally again and I wondered why Hope was so intent on not talking to me.

I soon arrived at the monorail station only to be greeted by the monorail speeding out of the station with Hope looking out the window. I sighed and sat down on a bench along the edge of the track. I looked around and saw the few people waiting. I took out my phone and went to the games section and started playing a dumb word game to pass time. However, I couldn't concentrate on the game and I kept losing. Why was Hope suddenly not talking to me? The question went through my head too many times to count. I came up with countless answers but none of them fit Hope's personality, and I doubted she would not talk to me for any of the reasons I came up with. I was thinking for so long I didn't notice the monorail rolling back into the station. As the doors opened a ding sounded.

Without even realizing I got up and walked on to the monorail. I was so lost in thought I didn't realize that it had only been fifteen minutes and the monorail wasn't going to the first ship and my home. When I got out of my musings I looked out the window, thinking about how in a few months I might see sky instead of space. The monorail wasn't open-air of course, it was protected by a double thick layer of Plexiglass all around to ensure the monorail wasn't sucked into the vacuum of space. It was at this point that I realized that the monorail wasn't going to my quarters, it was going to the third ship, where most food was produced and also there was storage. Since I didn't really find cans of oxygen, and food, or cows grazing interesting I didn't plan on getting out.

Luckily for me on the way back from the third ship of Nessie a broadcast came out of the monitors. It was the captain, and he had the cockpit in the background of the shot. He had his uniform on and he looked like a man about to tell a family of someone's death. He started to speak.

"We are having some problems with connecting the light engines and we may not start our trip towards Earth for another few days, but we will keep everyone posted, thank you." The message was short, yet eye-opening. If they said that they were having problems, the problems were pretty big. I was annoyed. The trip would probably not start for another week now or more. Ugh, I thought to myself.

When I got back to my quarters I got out lunch and while eating my sandwich I had an idea. I pulled out my phone and first made a contact for Bill and Hope, then called Hope. After two rings it went to voice mail, and so I called again. This time Hope answered on the first ring.

"What?" She said irritably.

"Whoa, calm down I just wanted to know why you were ignoring me." I said in a slow voice. "Look it's a bad time and I just need some time to think, okay?" She said. I started to ask her why it was a bad time but she hung up.

Ugh, girls these days. I mean, it wasn't like she had a job to go to right? I thought. Wait, I had a job that I had to resign. With that I put down with my sandwich and dashed out the door of my home.

The rest of the day went by quickly. I resigned my job, which (to be honest) wasn't hard at all. I worked out at a new gym in town and I talked to Hope for an hour about the DFF and predictions about what our first "assignment" would be. Aside from her bossy/irate side, Hope was actually pretty nice and funny. When we briefly talked about our days after the morning I got why she want to talk earlier. Apparently she had a lot of friends where she worked and it must've been hard for her to say goodbye. She must've been thinking about that on the way to the monorail and not talked to me for that reason. At the end of the day I reflected on the predictions for the first assignment and came up with some new ones. I was soon fast asleep.

Chapter Twelve
The First Assignment

The next morning I woke up late. Because I had quit my job, I hadn't felt the need to set my alarm. Luckily it was only 9:00, which would give me enough time to get there on time if I rushed.

On the monorail I was anticipating the first assignment. I was very nervous and yet excited. I had gone over the possibilities and I thought that most likely the first assignment would be some sort of training exercise for us. Some sort of test to determine how good we were. I speculated that it would be a test that all of the new recruits had to do. As it turned out, I was right.

I got to the maintenance-looking door on America street and Hope was already there waiting for me. She looked like she been waiting for some time, but I didn't care; I had to wait for her the last time I had been there. This time she opened the door for me and I walked inside in front of her.

"Have you had come with any more ideas about our assignment since last night?" she asked conversationally.

"Yeah, how about you?" I replied.

"Yeah, but you say yours first," She said, catching up to me.

"Well I think it's going to be some sort of test, maybe, instead of a training exercise. Though it might be both, I wouldn't know. " I shrugged. Hope nodded.

"I agree. I had a thought close to that, like a test or something. I guess we'll see soon though!" she said as we walked through the second door into the offices.

As soon as we got in I turned sharply and went towards the meeting room where I could see Mathers waiting for us. Hope seemed disoriented though, and shook her head for a second before turning towards the meeting room too. In a few steps I was opening the door and sitting down. Mathers still looked past me towards Hope, who was taking her time. I waited for a count of thirteen and then Hope got to the room and Mathers fired up.

"Your first assignment is a simulation. We need to know how you react under pressure and how you guys act as a team. This will determine how much and what kind of training you will receive. There is no way to fail in this simulation, so don't be worried." He stopped, obviously waiting for us to say something.

"What will the simulation be like?" Hope asked. Mathers smiled and replied, "we aren't going to tell you, how you deal with the element of surprise is also another factor. But I will tell you that there are three stages to this test. About half the people we have tested got past stage one. A small handful got past stage two, and none have passed stage three. So now just follow me to the simulation room." He finished and set off out the door towards someplace behind the cubicles. We followed him and saw there was a small room labeled simulator with two monitors and what looked like five helmets with dark glasses built into them.

We reached the room and Mathers opened the door for us. We could now see that on the monitor were controls for the simulation. Right then they only had the option to run the simulation, but I'm sure that once it was up and running they could monitor everything we did. Mathers stepped in and without saying a word picked up two of the helmets and offered them to us. I took the one on the right and put it on. It didn't look like much. In fact it didn't look like anything at all. I couldn't see anything.

"Right now both of you shouldn't be able to see anything. Can you?" asked the voice of Mathers. I nodded my head in answer.

"All right then. The simulation starts in five four three two one... Go!" He said.

Light flooded my helmet and I had to blink because the light was a little strong for my eyes. I scanned my surroundings. I was in the middle of a road in what seemed to be a city. Hope was to the right of me and if I wasn't wrong, above me was sky. I was in a simulated Earth. In front of us was a huge building that looked like it went up to the sky. I looked behind us and saw what I knew was called a car. It was moving as fast as the monorail towards us and I realized what was about to happen. I ran towards Hope and tackled her out of the road and out of the range of the car. I looked back and saw the car zoom past us. I let out my breath.

Hope looked angry at first, but saw the car going by and didn't say anything to me. We both got up and I turned towards the tall building. Suddenly words showed up where I was looking. I turned and they were still there. Hope must be seeing this too, I thought. The message read: 'stage two, infiltrate the One World Trade Center building. The building is heavily guarded and it is almost impossible to get in without an ID card. If you mange to get in go to the rooftop and more equipment and instructions will await you there.'

The message stayed on my display for a few more seconds then disappeared. I looked at Hope and by the look on her face I could tell she had read the message as well. She seemed to be sizing up the World Trade Center. I tapped her on the shoulder.

"We need to infiltrate the building here." She said, and pointed to the so called 'world trade center'. I nodded and didn't say anything.

"We'll need some identification to get in so..." She trailed off.

"Hmm..." I said and thought hard. I could maybe hack into their systems, but I didn't have access to a computer. This meant that we would have to find a place with public computers, so maybe a library I thought.

"Well I might be able to hack into their security but we have to have access to a computer, because if this is Earth, then phones didn't have the tools I would need to hack a security system. I was thinking we could maybe find some sort of library which might have a public computer." I said. Hope was frowning, until she reached into her pocket. Then a big smile lit up her face and she laughed. I looked at her questioningly and she spoke.

"We might be in a simulation of old Earth, but we still have our phones." She smiled, and pulled out her phone from her pocket. I smiled too, and pulled mine out.

"This just got a whole lot easier." I said, logging on to my phone and starting the browser. I typed in World Trade Center to the search bar and clicked search. Within seconds a picture of the building in front of us appeared along with a blueprint and a few sites about the World Trade Center. I clicked on the blueprint, which I couldn't see very well. The link took me to a website where the blueprint was very enlarged and I could click on parts to be enlarged even further and to give information. My smile grew wider at this and I handed my phone over to Hope who also went wide-eyed over the blueprint.

"This blueprint is good, but before planning how to get through to the roof, we need identification." She said intently.

I laughed. "When you have my phone, getting past security systems will be the easy part. " I said and exited the browser and opened the app I called calculator. Hope looked at the app and raised her eyebrows. It looked like a simple calculator but like N.E.S.S., it wasn't what it seemed. I put in the equation 3946 times 45. Then I turned the phone towards the ground and typed in a different equation without looking.

"Why aren't you showing me?" Hope asked.

"Well, it would be like telling you my password to my bank." I replied, still looking at the phone's screen, which was loading. Then a little bing sounded and I looked at Hope. "This is my best hacking software. One of my old friends programmed the app, but I created the software in high school. This will be able to crack the simulation system in seconds," I said, proudly. I clicked on button the menu for the hidden app, and waited for a second. Soon a option to hack appeared on screen and I clicked it. The loading screen appeared again and I turned to Hope.

"Will you look up people that work here on your phone?" I asked, and Hope looked bewildered. "I mean, just find some info about this place. My device can add our names to the database and make us seem like real workers or whatever but we need to know like background things. Like what kind of people do we need to be to get onto the roof, or at least the top floor of offices." I trailed off and sat down on the sidewalk. I laid down, waiting for Hope to say something. I counted thirty seconds, then a minute and Hope was still staring at her phone. I yawned and then Hope proclaimed, "Got it!", and I sat up.

"So what's the deal?" I asked her.

"There are two openings, or there should be for workers on the top floor. However we will be pretty far apart so we will have to really have a good plan." She put her phone on my lap and enlarged the top part of the blueprint. The spots were very far apart indeed.

"I think we should just go in and try to get on the rooftops," I said. "As long as we don't get caught, it shouldn't be that hard. Just be really obscure, like I transferred from Moscow or whatever the Capital was... or is I don't know. You can make up a good story. " I said, because I really didn't think it was going to be that hard at all.

I underestimated it.

"Actually, I've got a better plan." Hope said smiling and she started to tell me the plan.

Five minutes later Hope confidently walked into the One World Trade Center. We were going in separately in case one of us got caught, then the other could still get then out and or get to the roof. I checked my phone. It had been a minute. I strutted into the World Trade Center myself then, going over the plan in my head. I stepped into the line to get in and looked at the faces in front of me. They were calm and normal, and everyone was swiping their ID card and moving on. I molded my face to something like theirs and swiped my new fake ID card on the scanner. I took a deep breath and waited for the bing telling me to move on. I waited for what seemed like a minute until the beep sounded and I moved on. I let out my breath, calming myself briefly. My tech hadn't failed just yet.

Soon I was up on the top office floor. I tried to remember the way to my desk, but got horribly confused and ended up going to Hope's desk instead of mine. I saw her look at me sternly before turning around and heading the right way. Just don't act suspicious, I told myself as I walked past many regular workers. I soon reached the vacated desk that was now apparently mine. As I sat down in my chair a voice made me freeze.

"Who are you? I don't think I've seen you here before." Said a woman's suspicious voice. I spun around. The woman was blond and had on big glasses which made her raised eyebrows magnified.

"I... You wouldn't know me, because I'm new here." I stuttered. The woman looked confused for a second then smiled.

"Oh, well then nice to meet you. So will you be working the finances with us?" She asked, still smiling. I nodded and she stuck out her hand. I shook it and then sat back down and turned myself towards the computer on the desk. Trying not to look back at her I noticed how primitive the computer was. The monitor was connected to a big box of circuitry and the box went down to the floor. I was astounded by this and thought, didn't they have computers where half an inch of screen could hold the computer itself too yet? Wow, I thought. What would it be like if all computers weren't just thin screens and small keyboards? Snapping out of my musings I realized something.

This level wasn't the financial level. Either the woman was really dumb or I had just been caught. I almost slapped myself. She was probably calling security right now, I thought. So much for stealth, I thought. Hope's plan had just failed. I got up and bolted towards Hope. Chances were I already had security on me, so I thought that the best thing to do would to just try to get on the roof as fast as possible. I was sprinting now, and onlookers were bewildered as to why I was running. Soon I reached Hope's desk and saw her standing, looking just as bewildered as everybody else. She tried to say something like a whisper but I cut her off.

"Screw stealth! We need to get onto the roof ASAP! Security is coming, so lets go!" I said, not even trying to whisper. Hope hesitated for a brief second, then tore towards the maintenance room, which held a hatch to the roof. This had been the next step of our plan, but we didn't have a plan anymore. We had one word: run.

I ran towards the maintenance door and soon I was ahead of Hope. I slowed down enough to not hit the door and pulled it open. Hope barreled straight through and I followed her, with the door close behind me. The door slammed and I started up the ladder that Hope was already halfway up. I looked up and saw the light of the sun, and though I knew it was all simulated it felt real to me. I hoped that someday I could see this for real, and feel real heat. Still, I turned my thoughts back to the mission, or whatever it was.

I finished the climb and stood up on the top of the huge building, with the wind rushing across my face and hair, making it stick up. I looked at Hope with a raised eyebrow as if to ask her 'did we do something wrong?'. Hope seemed to catch my drift and shrugged, but no sooner had she done that then words appeared in front of me. They read: 'stage three: Jump.'

Chapter Thirteen
Touring and Training

I blinked. The message was still there. Jump. I looked at Hope who looked as disbelieving and bewildered as I'm sure I did. This could only mean to jump off the building. I slowly stepped towards the side and briefly looked off the edge before backing away. Jumping that would be very hard for me. It was scary enough to look at. I knew it was a simulation, but there something a little counterintuitive about jumping off a building. However, time was short and I heard shouts as security guards climbed up the ladder towards us. Soon we were all but surrounded with armed guards. I put my hands up and Hope did the same.

Then she did something that I didn't expect. She turned towards me and pushed me, probably as hard as she could. I was caught by surprise and I fell straight off building. I managed to look up and I saw Hope plummeting after me. I closed my eyes and waited for the simulation to end. I heard a long beep and then I opened my eyes. It was black but I heard the voice of Mathers again.

"You may take your helmets off now. As soon as you do I will show you the results." He said and I pulled the bulky helmet off my sweaty head. Mathers was standing next to his monitor where a bar graph was being shown. I walked over to him and looked behind me to where Hope was walking over towards us. I looked at the bar graph, it each bar was labeled as something they were testing for, but I didn't have time to read our stats before Mathers pushed a button on the computer and the stats disappeared and were replaced by a black screen.

"You did very well considering your age and experience. You passed the first stage, which worked on how you deal with situations with little time to think. You passed the second stage barely, though I think if you hadn't had your phones your tactics would've failed a lot quicker." Hope looked annoyed and Mathers nodded at her. "You have reason to be annoyed Hope. Jordan did not cary out your plan of being stealthy and unnoticed 'till you went to the roof. He tried, I think, to act normal around one of the workers who greeted him, but that didn't work." Mathers laughed. "Still you made it up to the roof and almost managed to complete stage three. " I cut him off.

"We followed the directions! How did we fail stage three?" I asked. Mathers shrugged and I rolled my eyes. Mathers began to talk again.

"The computer is still processing the results, and it does not lie. Tomorrow you will start your training that the computer recommends. Now you can leave, or go to the front desk to get your full tour of our offices and training facility." He then sat down at his desk and turned the computer back on. I sighed and turned around. I had no job other than this, so I decided to do the tour. I walked out of Mathers' office towards the front desk. The same woman from the day before was at the front desk, looking bored with the silence that surrounded us. The same people were at the desks, but they weren't yelling for files anymore, instead they were looking at random sites that I was pretty sure weren't work. One was looking at Chirper, and another looking at FacePage. For some reason they all were looking at social networks, but I turned away from them.

"Are you going to get the tour?" I asked Hope. She nodded.

"I mean, it's not like we have anything better to do." She said sadly. She was probably still sad that she had quit her job, even though I couldn't understand how she had so many friends from working maintenance. We got to the front desk and the woman looked up at us.

"Yes." She said in a bored voice.

"We're supposed to be getting the grand tour of this place," said Hope before I could speak. The woman's eyes seemed to light up at the prospect of doing something interesting.

"Ah, the tour. Finally something to do. I'll tell you the field workers get all the fun work." She said, in a envious voice. "Still let's start. As you probably already know this is the front desk, where I stay all day. In the middle are the computer geeks who never get any real work unless a big assignment is going on. Over there in the back right corner is Mathers' office, which you've already been in. In the opposite corner is the meeting room, which will lead us to the next part of the tour." She started towards the meeting room, looked at us and beckoned. We followed her. The meeting room looked the same as the day before with its high-tech screen on the table and the projector. The woman stopped and began again.

"This is the meeting room which, as I'm sure you can see, is equipped with the latest technology in projectors, touch screens, and even some holograms. This is where all assignments are delegated and where everybody meets to discuss intel. But now, for the good part. This door here goes to our training facilities, which will be the biggest part of the tour." She pointed to a door which was conspicuously painted the same color as the wall, yet I hadn't noticed it until she pointed. Then she opened the door and gestured for us to go in before her.

I stepped in first and was amazed. If the meeting room was high-tech, then this was the future. It looked like some sort of future arcade with holographic games and simulations, mixed with a fighting center. It had training places for fighters and even a small sparring ring. Some people were hitting bags with punches and crazy kicks, and some were standing wearing the same simulation helmets that we had used in Mathers' office. I was standing with an open mouth until the front desk woman started talking again.

"This is the training room. We have holographic games meant to simulate different skill training situation in the back. Right in front of you are customizable simulations which you might recognize from your initial test. Over across the room to the right we have our combat training. While it may not seem like a good thing to learn right now, if you'd ever been in the field you would want to start combat training. I've never been outside of this building for work, but almost all who have say the combat training is worth all the time it takes. Most likely, though you won't have the chance to start combat until you're finished at least two teamwork simulations and three different situations in the holographic games which we call holo-games.

Well, feel free to look around the place, just don't turn any of the holo-games on or the simulations." She smiled and turned to leave. I looked around again. I wondered what it would be like to train in here, wondered what the next day would bring.

24 hours later
****

"The first part of your training is a teamwork simulation." Said a uniformed man who looked like he had fought in a war, though there had never been any wars on N.E.S.S..

"You probably know the drill, so you will be in the simulation for two or more hours while we monitor you and then you will get a small break. Then you will go back in the simulation and we will repeat this until you finish at the end of the day." He led us to the nearest simulation station where the helmets were already ready for us to use. I took a deep breath then put the helmet on and faced the darkness. I heard Hope put the helmet on and immediately the screen lit up.

We were in what seemed to be a field. I tried to start walking, but my left foot wouldn't move. In fact, it seemed like I couldn't even move the whole left side of my body. I tried to close my eyes but only right eye would close. I tried pumping my arms, but only my right arm would move. Then I saw it, felt it. It was a weird feeling to see your body move not of your own accord. I saw my left arm move. It went in circles for a bit, then went back to its original position. Then it hit me: could I talk? I tried to yell and to my happiness it worked. Then I had another realization. Hope was controlling half of my body and I was controlling half of hers. At least that's what I thought. To test it I spoke to the air, hoping Hope could hear me.

"Hope?" I asked to what seemed the air in front of me. "Yes." I felt my own mouth move as the voice of Hope came out of my lips. "Am I right in saying that you are controlling half of my body?" I waited for the yes. "No." I was confused. "You're controlling half of mine." Hope said. I tried to think how that worked, but I remembered it was all simulated. I was sure they could've made me think I was in a giraffe body if they wanted me to. I tried to set my mind straight. We would have to be talking to each other a lot to act in unison, or at a different time in the case of walking.

"We need to act together," said Hope's voice, though I had been about to say the same thing. "Let's try walking," she said slowly. I took a step but so did Hope, making us fall on our backs. I let out a stifled "ow!" and heard the same thing from Hope.

"You go first this time," Hope told me, and I tried to nod my head but it didn't work. I put one leg up and Hope did the same a moment later. I pushed with the one hand I had control of and so did Hope, causing us to get back up. I stepped first this time, and Hope stepped after me.

"Okay, when I say one you take a step, and when I say two I'll take a step." Said the voice of Hope. "One," she paused as I took too big of a step for her and we toppled over again. I sighed. We slowly got up and tried to start walking again.

"One," she started and I took a step. "Two." She said and took a step herself. "One," I took a step, "Two." She took a step. "One, two. One, two. One, two." We were walking.

Hours later
****

I pulled off the helmet and leaned against the wall. I was hot and sweaty from wearing it for over four hours. I had just begun my second break and I was tired. Hope and I had managed to learn how to walk, which was first and easiest. We had learned how to turn around, which had taken almost half an hour and even then we could only turn slowly. Then guided by directions from the monitor people we had learned how to crawl, which was surprisingly easy, jump, which was by far the hardest, and finally learned how to swim, which was almost as hard as jumping. I knew from what the people had told us that the last session would be some sort of test on everything we done in the past two sessions. Hope came and laid back on the wall too and as she did I saw the man who had been monitoring us come out of one of the rooms in the back. He came towards us, smiling all the way, which made me very scared of what was coming next. He got to us, looking like a child going to the circus.

"The last part of your training is a test. You stumbled, fell, tripped and sometimes walked to get to this, but still you are well learned in the art of controlling half of one's body. Now all that you have learned will be put to the test in an obstacle course. Normally I'm sure this wouldn't be that hard for both of you, but now you will have to work together to finish in the best time possible. We've already programmed the obstacle course so whenever you are both ready you can go." He finished and turned to leave. As he walked back towards the control room I caught a glimpse of his face, which had the same excited look as before. I took a deep breath. An obstacle course, I thought, that couldn't be that hard. Then I remembered the past two sessions, and thought twice. My revised opinion was that it wouldn't be easy, but wouldn't be impossible.

I hesitated then walked back towards the station where the helmets were hanging in a taunting way, as if to say 'try me'. I sighed and secured the helmet on my head. I stared into the blackness and waited until I heard the sound of Hope getting up and coming to her helmet. I heard her put the helmet on and in a few seconds the simulation fired up. In place of the grassy field, there was a menacing, long obstacle course ahead of us. I couldn't see too many of the obstacles but the first few didn't look too hard. First there were four bars in our way that we could crawl under, a big wood wall with holds to climb up, and a small maze-looking obstacle that looked pretty confusing from the outside.

Already knowing the drill, I took the first step and I started counting in my head. One, two, one, two. The pattern went on in my head until we were running along towards the course and my feet went in time naturally.

"Crawl in three two one. Crawl!" Hope said and we dropped down to the ground in unison and started crawling under the bars. I tasted dirt in my mouth and almost coughed forgetting to get up as we reached the end of the first obstacle. However Hope didn't slow and got us up on one leg for a second until I realized my mistake and put my foot back down and took the first step towards the climbing wall. We got in our rhythm again until we reached the climbing wall. This was tricky, because we couldn't make a rhythm to our steps, and how we placed our hands, so we had to plan out the best route first. I quickly scanned the wall and planned out a quick easy route.

"To the left, up and then towards the right," I said, knowing from previous training that Hope would understand this. We slowly moved to the left then Hope got us up the first foothold, holding the one above. I put my foot out and very carefully placed it on the next hold, while Hope maneuvered to get closer to my side and higher. We went on like this, almost falling a couple times before finally reaching the top. At the top there was a ledge and a pole to slide down. Knowing that we had to slide down in order to keep a good time. I put my hand and leg on the pole and started to slide down as Hope and her side did the same. We got to the bottom and formed our rhythm again running at a fast pace into the maze. We had to slow down to take the turns but we managed to partially keep our rhythm going. Right, left, then we went left again, taking random turns until we hit a dead end and had to turn back. We kept going like this, hitting three dead ends until at last finishing.

In front of us was a completely different part of the course. There was a pool surrounded by fence closest to us, and behind the pool there was another wall, except this one was a lot lower and didn't have any holds. I was confused about the wall until it hit me: we had to jump up, grab hold of the ledge and pull ourselves up onto the wall. I was scared of how hard the wall would be but I started our running rhythm again and soon we were at the edge of the water.

I kneeled on my leg and Hope followed suit, then pulled her leg out from under us and out it in the water. From this we dived in to the freezing blue water and I was struck by the fact that though we were in simulation I could still feel the water soaking through my clothes and onto my body. I pushed my arm through the water, making us come up to the top briefly and it seemed that Hope blanked for a second and we sank until she did the stroke on her side. Then she started to kick and I tried but briefly forgot how to to kick with only one leg. Our rhythm was completely failing and we might as well have been doggy-paddling. Still, even doggy-paddling was swimming. Though we weren't doing it well, we were moving through the water. We kept doing our improvised stroke but seemed to be getting no closer to the end of the pool.

For hours, it seemed, we struggled, until finally I saw the wall straight ahead of us. I pulled my arm out of water on to the wall. A wave of tiredness hit me. As if the mental part of the challenge wasn't enough, I was tiring out now too. We slowly got out and I tried to start our rhythm of running again but I was too tired. Hope must've sensed this because she took the first step for me and I followed with my leg slowly. We started walking and I took deep breaths hoping that the next challenge would be easy. I looked up then and saw the wall again. I was stunned. How was I going to jump and much less pull my half up, I thought. Normally the challenge would be hard, taking me many tries, but in my state and with only half my body to use, the challenge would be practically impossible.

We continued to walk along, forgetting that we were timed. The wall was soon looming over our heads as if taunting us. The wall was smooth all the way up and I touched it as we got close to it only to find that it was very slippery, adding yet another thing to make sure we never got over the wall.

"We're going to have to get both of our hands on it to pull us up I think." I said to Hope. She put her hand in a thumbs-up to signal she understood. Almost in unison we bent our knees just like we had practiced and I held up one finger on my hand, then two and then three and we tried to jump. Just like so many other times in practice our legs were out of sync and we did a weird half-jump and crashed to ground. Both of us let out cries of pain as we fell, with me scraping most of the skin on my elbow off and Hope hitting her knee hard.

We got up and began to try again but it wasn't until our fifth try that we jumped in unison and Hope got her hand clinging to the top. However before I could get my hand onto the ledge as well Hope fell and we hit the pavement again. I was hurting. I just wanted it all to be over. We positioned ourselves for the sixth time. We bent down and I counted to three on my hands with my eye closed. We got it right again and I opened my eyes to see the ledge in front of me. I stuck out my hand and grabbed it then looked to see that Hope had too. I smiled and used the last bit of my strength to pull us up and onto the top of the wall. I looked up towards the simulated sky and smiled. We had done it.

Chapter Fourteen
The Final Simulation

The helmet's display went black and I was back in the real world. I took off the helmet and almost fell back onto the wall. My hair was soaking in sweat, my face was grimy and sweaty as well, and I was exhausted. The man who had been running our simulation looked satisfied, and maybe even proud as he walked over to me. He got to me, and Hope, who looked just as tired as I was, came over from the part of wall she was resting on.

"Though you did take a considerably long time in pool, your fast thinking everywhere else, especially the final wall which took most people many minutes to get across, made you get the second fastest time we've ever seen on this test! Congratulations on your time of 9:51," he said, looking proud. I smiled and sat down with my back against the wall. Though we had gotten through in less than ten minutes, when were in the obstacle course the minutes had seemed like hours. I looked at the clock on the far wall and saw to my surprise that it was 7:16 P.M., hours after we had started the simulation training. I tried to get off the wall but out of instinct I only used one leg waiting for someone else to move my other one. Hope was watching this and laughed. I joined her in laughing, then went back to leaning on the wall.

Over the next week we became known in the training rooms as one of the best teams around. We did another teamwork simulation and two holo-games, and in the second one we found that we practically thought in a team. Sometimes it seemed we had a telepathic link because of how much we could work together, think the same things, and even tell what the other was thinking sometimes. For the third and final holo-game we had the teamwork/stealth situation. We were in the holographic world where a man was standing next to Hope and me.

"Your final situation is the hardest one in the book. We aren't going to tell you anything about this except for three things. First, you will have ten seconds to decide what to do and which of the paths to take. Second, your mission is to get out alive. Last, you must both make it out to pass this. The terrain will appear in three seconds. Good luck."

He melted away, and as he did the terrain appeared around us. I took a quick look around. It looked like we were in a empty office, but what made me realize the situation was the label on the door. The label read: Will Greene, and under that there was: Top secret operations director. We were inside some sort of secret headquarters. I turned to Hope, who was staring at the name plate with her mouth open.

"We need to do something quickly." I said and Hope nodded. I wondered what would happen in ten seconds and looked at Hope who was most likely thinking the same thing. She turned to me and started speaking fast and showing her ability to think the same thing as I was.

"Probably because an alarm will go off in ten seconds or guards will come in. It probably has something to do with people finding us so we have to hide." She finished and I almost ran to desk to hide but stopped.

"No I hide you stay out." I said and had just enough time before ducking under the desk to see the look of understanding begin to dawn on Hope's face. I nestled myself under the desk just in time to settle down and stop moving before the guards came in. They were all holding knives and were wearing body armor. I took deep breaths and tried to be as quiet as possible while Hope told a story of how she had gotten put deep into the building by a weird man and had been looking for someone to help her find the exit. The story wasn't too convincing but it was good considering the short time it had taken to think up. The guards didn't sound completely satisfied when they began to speak, but they weren't arresting or her or anything.

"Okay, we'll show you the exit but just to prove you're not spying on our inner workings, can you empty your pockets for us?" I heard them say. I tried to think if Hope had anything that could make them know she was spying, but then I remembered all she would have was her phone. I hoped it wouldn't do anything to convict her. It was hard not being able to see what was happening since I was behind the desk, but judging by the silence I guessed that they hadn't found any bad information on Hope in her phone. I heard them begin to walk and let out my breath. I slowly tried to pull myself out of my hiding spot without making any noise so that the guards wouldn't see or find me.

I stood up and saw the guards in a sort of circle around Hope leading her out into a tight hallway lined with offices. Slowly I began to creep along behind them trying not to breathe loudly. Inside I was practically praying that no one would come out of their offices and see me, creeping along behind the guards, obviously trying not to be heard. To my luck no one came out and soon we reached what looked like a lobby. It was a huge room with a few desks and entrances to other hallways. The floor was lined with marble tiles and the wall was a dark hue of green. If I hadn't known better, I would've thought this was just a normal business.

As I looked around the room I realized how easily the supposedly hard holographic situation was coming. However no sooner did I think this than I tripped over a slight incline which I would've noticed if I hadn't been admiring the room. I hit the ground hard and loud, making the guards turn around to see me lying on the ground. My mind raced and I came up with the alibi that I was new to the job. I pulled myself up to find the face of a guard raising his eyebrow and looking very suspicious.

"Watch your step there, buddy," he said in a nice voice and my heart jumped hoping that he wouldn't press further. "Are you here for an interview or something? Because they are over that way." The guard gestured off to his left. Thinking quickly I shook my head and stuttered for a second before speaking.

"I... I... I work here and I'm on way out." I stated quickly and then turned and walked in the direction the guards and Hope were going, not even looking to see if there was a door ahead, but looking at my shoes.

"Wait!" One of the guards, a different one this time, yelled at me. I stopped in my tracks and turned to face them. One had a phone to his ear and had his out as if to stop me. He hesitated then spoke again in a smaller tone. "Come back here. I want to ask you a few questions." My body tensed and froze. Could they have found out? I wondered.

In a split second Hope began sprinting towards me and the guards, caught by surprise, didn't react immediately. I didn't see them start to run though, because I turned around and began running in the same direction as Hope. I looked up and saw that there was a door, though it was dark on the other side so I couldn't tell if it was an exit or not. I thought we were going to make it, and we were just about to burst through the door when three chatting women came through the door and Hope and I ran flat into them at full speed. Hope knocked down the one she hit, which then made Hope fall on top of the woman, while I got lucky and only hit the side of one of the women. Still, I toppled down and hit my chest again.

"Watch where you're going! Jerks!" The woman I had hit yelled at me. She looked disgusted but I didn't even give her an apology because I was so focused on getting up and looking around.

The guards were right on our tails now and getting closer by the second. I bent down next to Hope and gave her my hand to help her get up but as I pulled her up the guards reached us. I sighed and the holographic world disintegrated.

We had failed. The man who had monitored us in all of our tests, Gray, was standing behind where the holo-world had been, in front of us.

"You did very well and though you didn't completely make it, you did pass enough to get into your next stage of training. Anyway, those guards were wielding weapons but there was a way you could've gotten out of that." He paused but when neither Hope nor I asked what this way was he continued.

"You could have fought those guards, maybe even from the very beginning. So, now that you have passed through us and learned teamwork, strategy and to cope with different situations, there is one more thing we can teach you and that is how to fight. Your fighting classes begin next week and will continue for two weeks. You've tomorrow and the weekend off, so enjoy your rest." He held out his hand for us to shake. I gave him a firm shake and so did Hope, then we turned to leave.

The next day
****

As I ate my nuggets for lunch I turned on my laptop to look at the news. I hadn't been really checking when I was doing the daily simulations or holo-games, so the only news I had heard was that after delaying it three times they were going to finally begin the trip to Earth on Saturday. I had been completely ignorant of all other news, and therefore of all the news about the DFF until I got on my laptop.

I went to the TNN news site and immediately was frozen by the top headline. It read: 'DFF takes stand. In a stunning turn of events, a small riot from the DFF outside one of the minor government offices turned big when five members of the DFF used mallets to smash all the windows and break down the door. The N.E.S.S. police department broke up the riot and is now searching for these five to arrest them on charges of...'

I didn't read further than that, but I had read enough. Pictures from the riot made it clear just how crazy it had been. People were running everywhere, and in one picture you could even make out a masked man smashing out a window in the background. Under the article there was a link and a caption saying that the link was to the DFF website where they were openly showing how to join, though they denied that they were harboring the criminals who had smashed the windows. I clicked the link. The website opened up and immediately a video began to play. The video was of the DFF director talking to the camera in front of a picture of the N.E.S.S. ship. I heard him begin to talk and turned up the volume so his voice filled the room.

"Hello. My name is Ray Blackworth and I'm the leader of the Democratic Freedom Fighters. We are a movement dedicated to leading N.E.S.S. into a brighter and better future. Currently our government is breaking down. Beside the fact that it was a corrupt system to begin with, it can't follow its own rules, and it can't make a decision which is one of its biggest jobs.

But there is a way to abolish this ridiculousness. Join the DFF today and together we will build a society without the council. Together we will fly into a better future." The screen faded to black and the video ended, leaving me with the DFF website to look at. On the top there were four different tabs labeled: home, join, news, and help. Intrigued, I clicked the join tab which took me to a whole different screen which had places to put in name, address, phone, and surveys on how active a member I would be.

I leaned back in my chair and stared into space, thinking. If I hadn't been working against them, I would've considered siding with them. However, I was working against them, and judging from the way Mathers had talked about the DFF, their intentions were anything but peaceful. I was slightly bored so I finished my lunch and got up, then went out my door towards the monorail station.

Twenty minutes later I stepped off the monorail into the station, where there seemed to be an abnormal number of people, even for a Friday at lunch time. The station was packed to the brim with barely any space to move. Then I noticed that something was really off. No one was getting on the train. Everyone who had been on with me had either left or stayed on, but none of the people who were crowding the station was getting on the train. I pulled out my phone and dialed 3, my new speed dial for Hope, then put the phone to my ear. It rang three times and then Hope picked up.

"What's up?" She asked in a slightly loud voice, though I could still hear clanging and talking in the background.

"There something weird going on at the monorail station in the second ship. Where are you? You might want to see this." I said in a voice that I hoped conveyed my emotions to her.

"I'm in the bagel shop on America street so I'll be there in a few minutes. What is it though? You sound pretty serious." I knew she had gotten by my tone that this was serious.

"The station is more crowded than I have ever seen it, but nobody is getting on the monorail. I don't know if you have heard about the-"she cut me off.

"I know, this might be another riot. I'm heading towards you right now. I hope this doesn't get violent. Bye." She hung up and I looked around again.

The monorail was beginning to leave with barely anyone on it and more people in the station than ever, and though I couldn't see any people who were identifiably DFF yet, I was starting to think that this was going to be a bad riot or protest. My fears were strengthened when it seemed a new wave of people came through the doors of the station. I squinted and made out Hope in what seemed this new wave. I began to push through the crowd towards her, but as I did a voice rang out through the crowd. I turned around to see who and to my surprise and horror I saw Ray Blackworth standing in the middle of the station with a microphone connected to huge speakers next to him.

"Fellow people," he addressed us. I quickly fumbled with my phone to get the camera on and to start videoing the scene. "Most of you are here because you are fellow DFF members but some are just by chance. To you non DFF members welcome to our gathering, and to all returners welcome back to another 'meeting.'" He smiled in what I thought a devilish way, then launched into his speech.

"Here we stand at the monorail station. A place where we meet. A place that connects the three ships and connects us. Today we are connected to a very bad thing, though. A very bad thing indeed. Your very own government is the definition of corruption right now and we can fix that. Together we disconnect what needs to be disconnected and then connect back into a better, more whole society."

He paused as a chant of 'disconnect the council' rose out of the crowd. I was still frozen with my phone catching everything on camera and hoping that nothing violent was going to happen. Someone who was at the front out of the crowd next to Ray handed him a poster which said: disconnect the council to reconnect us. Then he picked up a hammer and some nails from the floor next to him and began to walk through the crowd towards the time schedule which was on a pole coming out of the floor. The crowd around him parted as he reached the pole. He held the poster steady and then began nailing it to the pole on the opposite side of the times. As he did this my eyes were drawn to the monorail arriving back at the station and the few that were on it getting off.

"Disconnect the system!" Ray Blackworth yelled and smashed the glass surrounding the monorail times and ripped the paper off. Then, he walked on to the monorail with everyone going behind him. The monorail left right after that and the station was in chaos. People were all trying to get out and go different directions while others were shouting for loved ones. Shards of glass were strewn over the ground. Unlike others, I however, just let myself go where the crowd was going, which was out of the station. As I was pushed, shoved, and kicked I felt my phone in my pocket vibrating. I pulled it out to see a text from Hope.

It read: it's chaos in here meet me @ the bagel shop on America street. I put my phone back in my pocket then stood on my tip-toes to see how far it was until I got out of the crowd.

I was almost to the end of the station. Soon I was at the beginning of the loop and then the crowd began to disperse into separate ways and finally I didn't have the people constantly bumping into me.

The bagel shop that Hope was talking about was fairly far down America street but not too far, so I got there in only about eight minutes. Hope was sitting in the window eating a bagel with a tired and slightly bored look on her face. She looked up when she saw me though, and suddenly looked wide awake. A bell on the door made a little chime as I walked in and sat down at Hope's booth at the window.

"I'm glad they didn't break as much this time. I actually thought they were going to do something worse." I told her and she nodded.

"What did you think they were going to do? Kill someone?" She asked.

"I don't know. I just thought that nothing good could come of another DFF 'gathering'" I said making air-quotes with the word gathering.

"I was thinking sort of thinking along the same lines when I saw this was DFF. Still, I just hope they don't do anything like what you said in the future. Then again, if they do it will be our job to stop it," she said thoughtfully.

"Yeah. Something like that." I said and with that Hope changed the topic and we began to talk about anything other than the DFF and our new job.

*****one day later.*****

It was a historic moment for N.E.S.S. on Saturday. We were finally starting our trip to the coordinates of Earth. The light engines had finally been installed into our systems and were going to start in a few minutes. I sat on my bed looking out the window at the endlessness of space. My laptop was on the bed sitting next to where I had been watching the live feed from the cockpit where they were doing final checks. I looked back at the computer screen to see the commander look at the camera in a solemn way. They then began to count down from ten. Nine, eight, seven, six. I looked at the pattern of stars in my window knowing that in a few seconds they would be gone. Five seconds until my life would change. Five, four, three, the pilot said 'lets go' in an undertone. Two, one, the pilot pressed a button and there was a jolt that knocked me off my bed. I quickly stood up and looked out the window to see the stars rushing by N.E.S.S.

We were finally doing it. N.E.S.S. was going back to Earth.

Chapter Fifteen
The Takeover

The next day was very boring. After a week of intense simulations and holo-games, life on N.E.S.S. didn't seem really as interesting as it used to be. The day went by slow and I often spent minutes looking out my window watching the stars go by and thinking. Finally, though, Monday came.

At 9:15 I walked into the old looking door at #46 America street with Hope right behind me. We walked down the old hallway and then into the headquarters. Then to training room, past the simulations, past the holo-games to the fighting training. A young man who looked only a few years older than me stood at the end of the room wearing a white robe and looking at us in a peaceful fashion.

"Hello and welcome to fight training. My name is Miguel Rivera and I'll be your teacher this next week." He smiled, making a good impression on at least me, and it seemed, on Hope too. He motioned for us to come in and on to the mats. Hope began to come on to them but quickly stepped off and took off her shoes and socks. I did the same the stepped onto the mats along with Hope. Miguel stepped towards us and started to speak.

"Punch me,." he said with a sly smile on his face. I raised my eyebrows, but Hope shrugged her shoulders, then threw a half-hearted punch at Miguel. He immediately went into a tense stance and blocked her punch, grabbed her arm and pulled her to the ground. He had her in a position so she was completely unprotected and beaten.

"I said punch me. C'mon try." This time he directed his command at me. I took a deep breath and threw a fast and hard punch at Miguel. He caught me mid-punch but I was ready for him. I pulled my arm back and in doing so pulled him towards me. I round-kicked him and tried to pin him, down but he used my arm to flip me over onto the mat and pin me down like he did with Hope.

"Good try. It seems you already know something, unlike her," he pointed to Hope. "But I don't blame her because fighting isn't exactly a common skill to have. I'm interested as to how you got at least a bit of training in this." He looked at me questioningly.

"I did karate as a kid. It was nothing big but I got kinda far and some of it stuck, I guess," I said, shrugging. Miguel nodded and looked pretty impressed. "Well, then I'll just start you a little bit ahead of you." He pointed to me and then Hope while talking. "However, both of you will always start and end the day with stretches and exercises to help get you in shape. Let's begin," he said, and with that our training began.

Every day, as Miguel instructed, we would stretch out then do sit-ups, push-ups, crunches and other exercises. Then

Hope would start with her basic punches, kicks, blocks and combinations, while I did a little more advanced work. We practiced and learned for hours on end, just getting farther along. We took a break for lunch in a shop across the #46 and I realized how fast Hope was going. She was almost where I had been an hour ago without any previous training. After eating lunch and taking a half-hour rest, we went back and kept on training.

At the end of the day, and the end of my energy, Miguel stopped us. I looked over to Hope to see that, like me, she was drenched in sweat. I leaned back onto the wall and then slid down so I was sitting on the mats.

"Get up you two! The hardest part of the day comes now, before your evening stretches, so get ready because you are about to spar!" he said loudly, and Hope looked at Miguel with one eyebrow raised.

"What the heck is sparring?" She asked, confused.

"Fighting. You'll put on some protection and then fight. We will do this at the end of every day, and then on the last day you will fight each other and then me," he said, smiling. I sighed, thinking about fighting Hope.

That first day I beat Hope. Yet, the next day she beat me. The next day she beat me again. Then I beat her two days in a row. Then she beat me once. I wasn't really counting but I was pretty sure we were even in wins and losses.

Also as the days went on our fights became more and more advanced. Soon we were not only using combinations and moves that Miguel had taught us, but a little bit of our own improvised moves too.

It was late on the last day when we were working on fighting an enemy with a weapon. He said this would be the most likely person that we would be fighting because DFF apparently often carried makeshift weapons. Hope and I had both learned and been tested on all Miguel's moves, so now we were both at almost the same spot, taking turns using Miguel as our armed dummy. He wasn't making himself too much of a challenge, just letting us get the feel for fighting an armed enemy so that we wouldn't make as many mistakes when he started fighting hard with his bat. I went and got some water from a bottle I had begun to bring while it was Hope's turn beating up Miguel. I finished my water and turned to see Miguel getting up off the floor with Hope standing over him. He got up, shook his long hair out of his eyes, and began to talk.

"I think you both have got the hang of fighting with a weapon against you so just if you're fighting them remember my tips, okay?" We nodded, and he continued. "Now it's time for the final three fights. First up, the final fight between you two. Get ready, and get pumped! Imagine this as a sort of championship." He finished and looked at both of us. We were watching each other closely, as if taunting each other non-verbally. I was the first though to turn to go and get my pads. I got there and slowly pulled my pads and gear on, preparing myself mentally for the fights to come.

A few minutes later I was standing five steps away from Hope, our backs turned away from each other. Miguel stood, silently counting down on his fingers from ten. All too soon it seemed Miguel shouted "go," and I turned around to face Hope.

We circled each other for the first thirty seconds, wondering who would throw the first punch or kick. I acted like I was going to try to punch and I knew Hope had seen this so then when she came to block me I kicked her instead and used her block hand to pull her so she had her back to me. Yet she seemed ready for this, because she then spun around fast and punched me very hard. I was knocked back a bit but I recovered fairly quickly. Hope then tried to kick me again, but I caught her foot and pushed her onto the ground. I thought for a split second that I had her, but then before I could pin her she rolled onto her stomach and jumped back up. I tried to do a very fast punch-kick-punch combination but only the second punch landed because Hope blocked the other one and the kick. Using my foot she got me to the ground and kneeled down to pin me. In split second thinking, I used my last resort: an improvised move I called the plus one. I punched across her face, intentionally missing her and then I punched up, hitting her chin, making a plus sign in front of my face and catching her off guard. She seemed to be slightly disoriented for a bit and she stayed on the ground. She got up soon but from that point she didn't seem as hard. I punched her a couple times and she just took it. I even did a few combinations and she didn't block most of the moves in them. She tried to hit me then, but all of her moves seemed feeble. She got sloppy to the point where she made a bad kick and I got her to the ground and pinned her. Miguel blew his whistle and the fight was over. I backed off Hope and laid back parallel to her. Miguel was clapping.

"Very good you two! Great moves, though I do admit that combo that Jordan did really messed you up, Hope. Are you okay?" He asked, concerned. Hope nodded.

"I'll be fine. I just need to take it slow for a bit. Why don't you two fight and I'll watch for a while." She sat down at the edge of the mats and watched us as we got ready, though I was practically ready so it was just me waiting for Miguel. Just then the woman from the front desk burst in with eyes the size of flying saucers.

"You have to come here fast! There's something going on. This is really big! Come now!" She said loudly and motioned with her hands for us to come. She looked really spooked by whatever it was so I ran towards her and out the door into the main room. There was a tv on the wall that I hadn't noticed before but it was now blaring the news. I looked at the screen to see what it was and my mouth dropped open. The two newscasters were talking very fast and the headline on screen was: DFF storms second and third floors of first ship, threatening violence.

"Yes, we got a call from a man who had apparently seen 'armed guards telling him to move out of his house and other guards doing this to others. Apparently this is going on in both the second and third floors. We even got this video sent to us a few minutes ago," the newscaster said, and a video of the third floor hallway showed up. The place was obviously very chaotic. Armed DFF members in the background were going up to doors, while the in main part of the hallway people were trying to get out with their belongings all around. The camera panned around and then the screen went black. I felt Miguel and Hope come next to me to watch, but I had seen enough. I began to walk towards the door, but as I did Hope ran after me to go with me.

"Hey, wait up! You know I live on the third floor, right?" she asked, catching up to me. I nodded. "Well," she looked at her watch, "if we hurry we could catch the afternoon monorail and get my stuff out. Oh, and by the way could I camp out at your place tonight seeing as you won't have your quarters taken over by DFF?" She smiled and looked at me with puppy dog eyes in a 'please say yes' way.

"Ugh. Maybe. I might not have room for you though cause Andreas is already staying at my place." Hope looked confused.

"But, he hasn't asked you yet. How do you know he needs somewhere to stay?" Hope asked. I looked at her with a raised eyebrow.

"Andreas lives on the second floor, so he needs a place to stay and unlike you he doesn't need to ask." This shut her up and I looked around the see that without thinking Hope and I had made it almost all the monorail station.

Soon we were speeding along towards the first ship and the chaos of the DFF. The stars were rushing by fast and we were coming ever closer to Earth. The monorail came to a halt minutes later and Hope and I stepped off to see a huge crowd of people with giant luggage bags trying to get on. As the last of us got off people began to swarm the doors and I got bumped into multiple times. As if it wasn't hard enough to not bump into people I also had to try and keep track of Hope. Eventually, we got out of the crowd and into the first floor of homes. I turned the corner and began walking towards the stairway with Hope beginning to run to get to the stairs. I began to run too and in the next minute we reached the stairwell. I pulled open the door and together we scrambled up the two flights of the stairs then down the hallway past the DFF officers and down another hallway after a right turn. Soon we were at Hope's quarters, where a DFF man was knocking on her door yelling for her to open up. We stopped at him and Hope tried to get in a couple breaths before speaking.

"I'm sorry sir, I live in there. May I go in?" She asked sounding very innocent. The man turned around to get a good look at Hope.

"Go in, get your stuff and get out! This is DFF property now!" he said, trying to sound intimidating.

"Isn't that illegal?" Hope asked, still trying to sound innocent.

"Don't worry about it, okay?" he said getting louder on each word. Hope, being the perfect actor, took one look at the blade in the man's hands and looked very scared by the prospect of a man with a weapon. Of course, she could have used surprise to disarm him and beat him easily in a fight, but that wasn't the best thing to do when there were so many other DFF guards around.

Still acting intimidated, Hope pulled out her key and unlocked the door. She then opened it and ushered me in to help her. Slowly but surely we packed her bags and then lugged them out one by one while the DFF guard stood patiently outside. Finally, fifteen minutes later we hauled out the last trunk, and closed the door to Hope's quarters. I took two bags and Hope took three bags, though it was really two because her backpack weighed nothing. The third floor looked nothing like it had in the video. The initial craziness of the takeover had calmed down and now the DFF guards were all just talking in a circle until they heard us coming towards them and parted for us. Taking the rolling suitcases down the stairs was a bit hard but we managed and in the end we got back to my quarters where we stopped. I pulled out my key and unlocked the door, then opened it to find Andreas sitting on the couch eating chips and watching a movie.

"Hey Andreas," I yelled over the sounds of the movie. He looked up and grabbed the remote to turn the volume down.

"Hey man, is it okay if I crash here for the night?" he asked, turning back to the movie.

"Course it is, but Hope is also staying the night here because she lives on the third floor so I guess you guys can decide who sleeps on the couch and who sleeps on the floor." I began to pull Hope's bags in through the door. Hope did the same and as she did Andreas looked up again from his movie towards Hope.

"You can have the couch. I have a sleeping bag, so I'll be fine on the floor," he told Hope and as if to show this he moved from the couch to the floor. My quarters were packed with people and bags that night, though I was still happy that I didn't get forcibly removed from my home by the DFF.

The next day started out pretty crazily. Half asleep, I had to navigate my way through the piles of luggage, wake up Hope and Andreas, then navigate all the way back to my kitchen so we could have some breakfast. After breakfast we went on the monorail, which was equally crazy, with lots of luggage from people still sleeping on the monorail because they had no place to go for the night. Most of the seats had already been taken by sleepers and so Hope and I had to stand near the doors in the middle of suitcase city. It seemed like the whole ship was still in shock from the DFF takeover. After minutes of awkwardness trying not to step on anyone's trunks the monorail came to a halt, the doors opened, and Hope and I exited. The station was also lined with sleeping bags and suitcases, but they were not as tightly packed as inside the monorail.

In a few minutes more we were back into #46 America street where the woman at the front desk told us that we were done training and now we would be briefed inside the meeting room on gathered information and meet the rest of the teams. In the meeting room, Mathers was already at the head of the table typing on a computer. There were two empty seats at the end of the table and all the others were taken by people who I had never seen before so I assumed they were the other teams. The door closed behind us and Mathers looked up to see us sitting down.

"Ah, here we are. Everybody meet our newest team Hope Hoffman and Jordan Thorne. Now, before we recap all our current information for them please go around in your teams and introduce yourselves." He motioned to us. They then began to go around and introduce themselves. The first team was made up of a woman whose name was Claire and had hair that was an unnatural shade of red, and a man named Alex who looked like he was almost seven feet tall. The next team was a pair of identical twins named Ben and Harrison. The third team was made up of a woman named Katia and a woman named Kate. The second to last team was made up of a man named Joey who had a smile that made me want to smile too, and a woman named Isabella. The final team, sitting next to us, was a man named Jasper whose hair was jelled up in the front, and a woman named Skyler. After they had all introduced themselves, Mathers began again.

"Great, now that we're introduced we can begin." A PowerTip appeared on the screen behind him titled: current info on DFF operations. He started to go through the slides and told us about each one of them.

"One of our biggest objectives used to be to find out where their main base of operations was, because we only knew where one of their minor bases was. However, as of yesterday they've made themselves a new main base, which they aren't doing a very good job of hiding. Still, this has gotten us to our next step, which will be to map out and infiltrate the second and third floors of the first ship to see what they are planning. Now, you may think that we haven't done anything, but we gathered some substantial information on the DFF so far. For one thing, we know that their intentions are anything but peaceful and they intend to completely destroy the council in whatever way possible. We also know that they plan to make some sort of new weapon that would render them unstoppable. We know that they're trying to gain members, but that isn't a fact that they are trying to hide in anyway. So most of you teams, including our new team, will be working on a 3-D holographic map of the second and third floors. Of course we can access the Nessie database and find a map, but we also need to map out all possible entry and exit points. Then you'll go into the field to see where the DFF members will be guarding so we can mark that on the map. Now, as for Jasper and Skyler, you two will be doing surveillance on the DFF outpost. Now go and stop the DFF!"

He finished and the PowerTip ended. He closed his computer and picked it up to leave. At the door he turned around and pressed a button on the side of table. A hologram then appeared in the middle of the table of the second and third floor of homes. Also there was a screen for each seat which had a 2-D model of the floors which each of us could edit. I looked up at the 3-D model where all the stairways had already been labeled as the obvious entry and exit ways. Soon after this, Joey stood up and Isabella did too.

"Well, if we're ever going to get this map done at least one or two teams have to go see where the DFF is guarding. So, I volunteer myself, Isabella, Hope, and..." He paused pointing at me, trying to remember my name. "... Jordan?" he asked, and I nodded, making him fist pump the air.

"I knew it! Anyway you guys should come with us to get a sense of what it's like out in the field, it will be a good initiation for you guys. C'mon lets go, if we run we could still make the 10:00 monorail back to the first ship. " He grabbed a jacket and Isabella also stood up and motioned for us to follow her lead. Both of them went to the door and I snapped out of the trance I was in. I got up and went to the door with Hope right behind me. A minute later we began to jog along America street.

When we reached the first ship and the hallway that my quarters were in, Isabella stopped us. She told us that we would have to try to get in through whatever security and get something out of our quarters or some dumb story like that. The main thing was to note what kind of security they had and where it was. Joey had the idea to split our teams up for the two floors so each team would have one experienced person to show the other how to get in. We agreed to do this and then split, with Joey and I together, and Hope and Isabella together. Joey had a room on the third floor and Isabella's quarters were on the second floor so it worked out perfectly. We went in to the stairwell and waited for Isabella and Hope to go up the first flight of stairs before going so we wouldn't look too suspicious. We slowly walked up the two flights of stairs and as we did, Joey began to speak in an undertone to me.

"Listen up. We're going to have to pretend to be something. How about... Uhh friends and I left your laptop in my quarters because I was scrambling to get my stuff last night, and now you need it so we need to go get it. Try to act a bit mad at me, yet pleading to the guard," he said and I nodded. We had already passed the second floor and were heading up the final stretch of stairs. From there I could already see the guards at the door to the third floor, who stiffened when they saw us coming.

"What are you two doing here? This is DFF territory now," the guards said menacingly. I pretended to look scared by them and I began to talk.

"We'll, I'm sorry sir it's just that my friend here lives on the third floor and I left my laptop at his place yesterday morning and he forgot to get it out so now we have to get it because my laptop has all my work on it. So please can we just go in get my computer and go out, " I pleaded. They looked at each other and exchanged meaningful glances then replied.

"Fine, but we have to go with you. We'll go in, get your laptop and get out, got it?" I nodded and so did Joey. Then Joey pulled his key off a lanyard on his chest. The guards opened the door and we took a step into the DFF-occupied third floor. It looked the same, yet the whole place had a different air to it. I quickly scanned the room and saw that a few doors away one of the places was being guarded by four guards. I took this in then quickly looked to where Joey was going and where his quarters would be. We turned left and then went down the hall until we reached his quarters. Joey unlocked the door and we stepped inside. I didn't have to be a detective to realize that Joey's quarters were one of two things. Either Joey was just a really messy person, or his home had been ransacked. Books and paper were strewn everywhere, one of his lamps was turned on its side, and it looked like a cup of pens had been knocked over on his desk. Joey obviously had noticed this too and for a second a look of surprise showed on his face, but the look was gone just as soon it came. I focused on looking for a computer this time and spotted a blue laptop in the corner of his living room. I went and grabbed it then showed it to the guards. They nodded and we exited his home with the guards still flanking us. I tried to get one more good look at where the guards were near the door to the stairwell on the way out. I counted in my head four doors from the stairwell until the guarded one and took a mental picture of the hall. After that we exited the third floor, thanked the guards for their trouble then walked back down to the first floor where Isabella and Hope were waiting for us.

"We didn't get much. All we saw there was the DFF men guarding the doorway. Though actually there was one weird thing. When we got into my quarters it seemed messier than I remembered it," Isabella told us, sounding suspicious.

"Yeah, the same thing with Joey's home. I don't really know if you're that messy, but this looked like someone had deliberately ransacked his place. The thing I'm confused about is why would the DFF want to do that? I mean likely everybody packed everything important or valuable and even if they hadn't, why would the DFF need it?" I asked the room, confused. Both of the women nodded in a meaningful way, both thinking about my question. Joey, however, was still on other things.

"Well, unlike you guys, I actually saw something other than the door guards. I think it was four doors away from the flight of stairs there was a home being guarded by DFF so something's definitely going on up there. Anyway, I think we should get back to base and put all this on the map. Lets go," he ordered and motioned to the door. We nodded and began towards the door out.

Many minutes later we were back in the meeting room where most people were chatting aimlessly waiting for us to be back with information to help make the map. When everybody saw us, they sat up and looked attentively. Joey went to the front then, and recounted all the information we had gathered, which the teams eagerly put on the map. After all that was done we chatted for a few minutes and then Mathers came back in.

"It's been an hour and a half. Show me your progress so far." In response Alex pushed the hologram towards Mathers. He looked at it carefully then nodded, seeming slightly impressed. "Good work. Lunch break for all of you. Come back by 12:30 or you'll have double duty on surveillance." Everyone began to get up to leave. In the bustle someone yelled out, "It's Skyler's turn at Papa's." which made no sense to me until Joey told me what it meant.

"Every day we have lunch at Papa's pizza and we take turns paying for it. Today is Skyler's turn to pay, so if we add you two to the end of the list, you'll pay in four or five days." I thought about it as we left the place and it seemed like a great idea. I was elated. We were going to lunch, which I didn't have to pay for, and I had just done a successful mission.

Chapter Sixteen
Infiltration Again

Three days passed without much happening. Hope and I learned just how boring 'surveillance' at the DFF outpost was. We had to watch the outpost for an hour and a half and make note of how many people went in and if any suspicious activity was going on that we could see. I almost fell asleep twice, and Hope had to pinch me to get me awake again. Other than that, we had found another door that the DFF men were guarding, but that was pretty much it.

On the fourth day, things got interesting. It was the beginning of the day and Mathers was in for his usual update, but he didn't have much to say. "Today we will start making the plan for getting into and finding what the DFF is guarding on the third floor." He told us, pointing to the fourth door from the stairs on the hologram which was labeled: guarded by two men. Mathers then left without another word and the room was silent for a few minutes until Hope spoke.

"Can one of you guys who knows how to work the hologram add the maintenance diagram onto this?" Across the table, Ben nodded and started to type something on his screen. Twenty seconds later a new part of the map, which was in green unlike the blue of the rest, showed a lot more. Suddenly Hope's eyes widened and she pointed to a spot on the green part of the map.

"There! I remember hearing about people having broken oxygen ducts and you would have to go in the duct to fix them. That's a perfect entrance into any room. Plus the guards are on the outside so they won't see us. We can just go in through say, Jordan's oxygen duct, and using this map someone who stays here can guide us to the room. It's a perfect plan!" she told us happily. Ben looked down at his screen and for a second the hologram disappeared, but when it came back Ben looked up with a smile on his face.

"It might just work!" he exclaimed. This seemed to spark a wave of emotion around the table as most began to smile and Isabella even clapped a few times for Hope.

"This seems pretty straightforward so I guess we should decide who's going," said Ben. "I, for one, volunteer to stay behind and monitor whoever is going and I think Harrison will too," he said, looking at his twin, who nodded in assent.

"Well, I think that since we have Hope to thank for this we should let her and Jordan go," Isabella said kindly. Most of the teams nodded and generally agreed. Though I didn't say anything, my insides were dancing the congo at the prospect of a mission. Anything to get out of the dullness of the past few days would be awesome.

"I also have a recommendation as to who should go," began Claire. "I think Katia and Kate should go because they haven't gone in a while, plus they are some of our best fighters, which could come in handy in this situation." There was a general murmur of assent.

"Well, then, if it's you four then I will go tell Mathers and you guys will be on your way. I'll also get the remote trackers and communication devices so we can monitor you and give you directions," said Harrison, then he stood up and walked out of the meeting room. I leaned back in my chair and stifled a yawn.

Soon Harrison was back with earpieces with which to talk to us and a tracker which we all attached to the sides of our pants. We each tapped the trackers in turn to turn them on, then headed out.

Twenty minutes later we were standing in my quarters with Hope hard at work, prying the oxygen duct open. After a few minutes she finally was able to dispatch the cover from the actual duct. One by one we bent down and crawled into the tiny duct. I hit my head twice just going in. Slowly, though we all got in and began bumping along, with Ben directing us through the maze. We went right and left through turns, and twice we reached a section where we had to climb up to a new floor of twists and turns.

After fifteen minutes of crawling and bumping each other Ben told us that the next right turn would lead us to the duct to the guarded room. I crawled along for a few more feet until we reached the turnoff to the grate of the guarded room. Then, because Hope was in the back and I was in the front of the line, I could only barely hear her say "This is it", but the words rang in my ears. I took a deep breath to calm myself and slowly turned..

We slowly moved along, just like before, except everybody, including myself, seemed tense, ready to move at a moment's notice. I put my hand back towards them as I got to the grate so they would stop. It was hard to make out the surroundings looking out from the grate, but I could definitely see a person, not a guard, looking an object I couldn't see on a table. The table was also strewn with papers, and the man seemed to be looking at a blueprint of something. I moved over onto my back with my foot towards the grate then slowly began to push on it. At first it seemed as stiff as if I was pushing on a tree, but then after a minute or so of straining my muscles, the pressure seemed to lessen. I pushed more and the grate began to slide forward, bringing a smile to my dirty face.

One minute and a lot more pushing later, the grate seemed to give up in its battle with my foot. I gave it one hard push, and the grate fell to the ground below with a clang. Without looking at the floor and room below me I pushed myself out of the duct and into the room. The immediate things I noticed were the things I couldn't see from behind the grate. First, the door was slightly ajar. Second, the man at the table had a knife at his side. And last, there had been guards waiting for us under the grate. We had been ratted out.

Both the guards who had been stationed under the grate were now looking at me menacingly, knives in hand. They advanced on me, but as they did I saw Katia climb out of the oxygen duct. Assessing the situation quickly, she hit both of the guards in the head with her tracker, making them sink to the ground for a few seconds before getting up. However, those few seconds were enough for me to snap out of my fear. They got up, going back to back in order to face both of us at the same time. I focused on my attacker and began to dodge and weave through the guard's swipes and swings. 'Wait until his guard is down then disarm the attacker so you are even,' said the voice of Miguel in my head. I waited and soon I saw the guard's defensive arm fall. I took this as my chance and in between one of his swipes I seized his weapon and pulled it from his grasp. I threw it to the floor, making yet another clang. Now the fight was even.

As I threw the blows of victory I could hear Miguel's voice in my head telling me the next move, and cheering me on. I threw a well aimed punch at his stomach, and the guard keeled over, unconscious. I looked at Katia who had already taken care of her attacker. She was doing battle with the man from the table who, judging by his movements, wasn't very adept at fighting. With one quick move, Katia pulled the blade out of the man's hands and banged the handle on his head, knocking him out.

"We have to get out of here now! Reinforcements could arrive any second!" shouted Katia. I nodded and Katia started climbing back into the duct. However, I stayed back, going over to see what the man was making. I got to the table and turned my head to look at the blueprint. At first I couldn't decipher what it all meant, then I put it all together in my head and a gruesome picture formed. Just as I was about to usher Katia back the door was slammed open by a group of four guards.

In that moment instinct took over my body and I ran towards the duct. I jumped up and pulled myself in as fast as I could, adrenaline coursing through my body. By the crazed look in my eyes Katia and the others understood that we had to leave. We crawled and crashed through the maze of ducts as if we were mice running from a big cat. Ben was shouting directions faster then ever in my ear, barely keeping up with our speed. After many hard turns and bumps that I would regret the next day, we made it back to the quarters. One by one we pulled ourselves out of my oxygen duct, covered in bumps and bruises.

"What happened?" asked Hope in a bewildered voice. "All I saw was Katia and Jordan going into the room telling us to wait, and then having to rush back here. What's going on?" she practically yelled. I took a few seconds to catch my breath then recounted all of what had happened to us. After this, Katia, who hadn't known about me looking at the blueprints seemed confused.

"But what was the blueprint for? You said you saw it but you didn't say what it was for," she asked. I nodded.

"I was about to get to that. This is the really scary part though. So, the blueprint was really weird and had all these parts you had to build but when I put them together in my mind it was... A... They're trying to make guns. It must've been why they were ransacking quarters. I think they were looking for parts. " My words made a silence close upon the four of us. It was truly horrible. Guns could kill, if not seriously injure, for this reason, guns were illegal to have aboard N.E.S.S. All we knew about them came from history books and pictures of war. If they were making guns, then who knew what they could've been planning. Everyone seemed to be in deep in thought.

Hope snapped out of it.

"C'mon guys I know it's a lot worse than we thought, but we have to get this back to base. According to Jordan, someone is a mole on our team so the DFF guards might come down here and try to get us. The longer we wait here the bigger chance there is of guards coming, so lets get back now!" She ushered us towards the door. We didn't say anything more, but we followed Hope out the door of my quarters and into the hallway, then the monorail station. I realized during all this that our earpieces didn't have microphones on them because Ben didn't hear us. All he could do was give us directions and monitor where we were. This made me wonder how Ben would know if we were in trouble, and I realized that he wouldn't be able to tell. When we were on the DFF-occupied floors, no one could help us.

A monorail ride and a bit of walking later we were back inside the base and were greeted with somewhat of a hero's welcome. Everyone was happy for us, giving smiles, and some giving a couple claps. We, however, did not return the smiles and the happiness. I tried to put on a smile though, and began to speak.

"So, there is good news and bad news. Which do you guys want to hear first?" There was a general ring of "good news first,", and so I went on to the good news.

"Well, we gathered a lot of new information." I paused, hoping it wouldn't sound that horrible.

"However, the bad news is basically all the information we gathered. First, there is a mole who sold us out. They knew we were coming and they knew where we were coming from. The guards from outside the door had been repositioned to under the grate, waiting for us. We could have gotten a lot more information if they hadn't known we were there. Luckily I did catch a glimpse of what they're doing, and it isn't pretty. They're in the early stages of building guns." I finished and all the warmth in the room seemed to be sucked up by my words. What we were left with was a cold dark atmosphere and silence.

Most people were just staring at me or the wall with open mouths and eyes as big as dinner plates. Harrison didn't seem to be concentrating on what he was doing, yet his hands were putting the information on our map and our computer database. I watched as he labeled the guarded room as 'gun factory' then he closed our blueprint of the second and third floor. He went to our DFF folder on his screen, which was facing me, and in our information document he added 'DFF is in early stages of making guns.' Then 'one of us is working for the DFF secretly' and closed the file, still not looking at what his hands had done.

While all this commotion, or lack thereof, was going on Mathers walked in. He looked grave, and I assumed he had heard, or had the updated information document.

"Saw the new information?" I asked him and he didn't look over to me but he nodded. He came into the middle of all us and started to speak.

"Everybody, I know you're a little shocked, but we need to come together again. We can definitely say now that the DFF doesn't have peaceful intentions at all. But we need to know more! We need to find out their plan, and stop them! As for this mole, I will put our newest members on the case to find and stop this mole, as they, Katia and Kate, could not have been the mole unless they disappeared to call their DFF friends at any time during the mission. " He looked at us four, and we shook our heads in response to his question. A few more seconds of silence passed, then the whole meeting room exploded into conversation. I turned to the door and ushered Hope to come with me. She wouldn't have been able to hear me in the meeting room, and I wasn't even sure I would have been able to hear myself. Outside the door I turned to Hope.

"So I guess our priority from now on is finding the mole or moles. I think we first need to know who knew about the mission. We can definitely say that everybody else who wasn't on the mission is a suspect." Hope nodded, though she was deep in thought.

"You're right, we do need to figure out who else knew. Mathers knew, so he too is a suspect. Now we have to just go around asking the other staff here if they knew about this mission." Hope started towards the front desk where the woman was looking at her screen in a slightly bored way. We got to her and Hope cleared her throat to alert the woman.

"Did you hear that the DFF are making guns now?! They just found it out on the latest mission into DFF territory," Hope said, in a gossiping voice. The woman looked up and nodded. "Yeah, Mathers got all the staff together and told us about the mission right after they left to go. I didn't know they were making guns though! That's horrible!" She said, in a disgusted voice. We walked away back towards the middle of the room, and Hope gave me a look of victory. "See, it's as easy as that. Now we know that every employee and worker here could be a double agent we can start," she said happily. I let out a big sigh. It was going to be a hard job.

Chapter Seventeen
Suspects and Progress

The next week passed without much advancement in our hunt for the mole. We only had gotten one suspect off our list but, as I kept telling myself, it was more than nothing. We had devoted one of the cubicles usually used for research on the DFF to our hunt. We had pictures posted of every worker with their named labeled except for us, Katia, Kate and Miguel who had been sick for three days, one of which was the day of the mission, so we had ruled him out.

We were sitting at the two chairs of the cubicle when it happened. We had been pretty much oblivious to what was going on elsewhere in the base, other than Mathers' daily updates, so it was a surprise to us when Ben came running over to us, looking scared and frantic.

"Guys I hope you're narrowing it down fast because something really bad has happened." He said, his voice sounding as frantic as he looked. His face fell as he saw the looks of guilt on our faces, but he continued.

"We sent out Alex and Claire to go do some reconnaissance around the second and third floors using the network of oxygen ducts, and it seemed to go fine until, judging by their trackers, they went out of the duct system in one of the second floor rooms, then slowly went out of that room and into the hallway and then into another room. If I didn't know any better I would say they were being pulled out of the room and into the other. Then they disappeared. Someone turned their trackers off and now they could be anywhere. We've lost them," he ended in a grave voice. He let this wash over us for a few seconds and in that moment I realized just how important finding this mole, this double-agent, this traitor was. They had taken our fellows. I let this sink into my head and my mind started to form a plan. Ben walked away towards the meeting room, still looking shaken and as the plan in my head became more and more formed I stood up.

"Hope, I have a plan. We can't investigate every one of our suspects fast, so we need a way to get a lot of people off our list at once and that's what I have in my mind. If this works well, we could cut our in list more than in half. If it doesn't, than oh well, but here it is. So tomorrow Katia and Kate will suggest that we go back to where they were making the guns because they're probably focusing their efforts on guarding wherever Alex and Claire are being hidden and not on the 'gun factory'. Everyone will agree, and Katia will go to tell Mathers, but instead of going to his office she will just go outside of the meeting room for a minute and then come back in and act as if she had told Mathers. So then if there aren't any guards under the oxygen duct grate then we will know that the mole isn't on any of the teams because if Mathers knows he'll tell everybody else." I finished and Hope looked impressed.

"What happens if there are guards there?" she asked. I thought for a moment then answered.

"That could mean one of two things: either the mole is in one of the teams, or they just kept guarding the place in case we came back. The first is more likely but we don't want to mess up in our search." Hope nodded and a smile began to appear on her face.

"That just might work," she said, the smile spreading all the way onto my face.

The next day we put the plan into action. The previous night we had told Katia and Kate about it. They had agreed to play their part and so within half an hour of Mathers' day-starting information recap to us and the other staff, we were all watching the holographic map. On it were Katia and Kate, symbolized by red blinking lights moving through the green duct system. We watched for a bit then went back to our own desk where we sat back. All we could do now was wait for the mission to be over.

Forty three minutes later my heart leaped as I saw Kate pull open the door to be greeted in the same way we had been when we came back from our mission through the ducts. Kate went over to greet the other teams, while Katia came over to us two.

"You guys got very lucky. There were no guards, so I guess you can cross off every team as a suspect," she said, elated. I smiled widely and looked back where 10 pictures and names were ready to be ripped off of the suspect list. I looked at Hope and she seemed to be reflecting my happiness right back at me. Together we carefully took off the pictures and names of all the teams. Now there were only four suspects left. There was the woman from the front desk whose name was Jean. There was Mathers. There was Gray, who had been our monitor during all the simulations and holo-games. Then there was one other monitor who was named Nikhil. It had worked. My plan had worked amazingly well and I was ecstatic about it.

The rest of the day went by pretty fast. Other than decimating our suspect list, Katia and Kate's mission had helped us gain some new information on what the DFF was doing. Judging by the blueprint Katia and Kate brought back, they were on their fourth prototype of their gun and we thought they must be very close to getting it right. We also found out that as soon as they perfected their gun design they were going to mass-produce them for whatever giant revolution they had in store for N.E.S.S., unless we could stop them.

Mathers was slightly mad at Katia for not telling him, but Katia said she had forgotten. Plus he wasn't too mad because of the information we had gathered, though we didn't tell him about narrowing down our suspects seeing as he still was one, and there was a 25% chance that he was the mole. I went home feeling satisfied with my day.

That night I had another crazy and stupid idea that I thought would narrow down our suspect list even more than we already had. I used my phone connected to my laptop to hack part of the N.E.S.S. database, which took a good hour, and then I searched for all information on Gray. The search took quite a while and I ended up reading for most of the time and then watching tv. Finally at 12:45 the search finished and I went, with my closing eyes, back to my laptop where all the information was overloading its hard drives. Some part of me asked myself why I was doing this but I ignored it. I skimmed over most of it but there was no connections to DFF at all. Even through all of his web records I couldn't find anything. Before falling asleep I deleted all the information off my computer and wondered if this meant we could take Gray off the suspect list.

I wasn't the only one who was tired at the next day's meeting. Hope was also putting her head down during Mathers' morning update. I think I might've even fell asleep once during the meeting because it seemed awfully short. When it ended, Hope and I both trudged to our desk and sat down with the same look of half-awake and half-asleep on our faces. I was the first to speak.

"I stayed up pretty late hacking all of N.E.S.S., but I don't think I found anything useful. I was trying to find out if Gray had any connection with the DFF, but I didn't find anything bad on him, so if he is the mole he is pretty good at hiding it," I said, stifling a yawn, then sighing. Hope suddenly seemed more alert though as she began to talk.

"Well, since not everyone can hack the whole ship's database, I just used Hoogle to search up some stuff. I researched the high ranking DFF people to see if they had any connections to our suspects. It took me a long time to do each DFF official, but eventually it paid off. It was this man, Edward Richards, and I was looking at his credentials and those sorts of things when I saw that he was married to a one Jean Longfellow. If there is one person who has a big connection with the DFF, it's her. Plus think how easy it would be to just message her husband about our missions. It has to be her."

I smiled. The week and a half of looking had finally paid off. My insides did a victory dance as we walked towards the front desk where Jean was looking as normal as ever typing something on her computer. Her face looked completely innocent. Hah! I thought, she must be guilty. We got over to her desk, both of us wearing triumphant looks.

"Give it up Jean! We know you have been giving our information to the DFF." Said Hope.

"Or should we call you Mrs. Richards?" I asked, raising my eyebrows at her. Jean sighed and looked up.

"I knew this would come up. Yes, I tried to hide it, okay. I *used* to be married to that psycho. However, I divorced him three years ago because he joined the DFF. I've always hated their views and though I was married to him once, I have no intention of giving up information to the DFF and I never have," she said in a sad, yet stern voice. My shoulders fell, and so did Hope's. we had been so sure that it was her, and it had seemed so true. Yet she had just gone from our #1 suspect to not even our list by the way she talked about her husband. I sighed a deep long sigh and turned back towards our desk. At least we were closer to finding the mole, I thought sadly. I had been so sure it was her, though. Maybe my mind was just looking for an answer after the week and a half of looking. Maybe I was just tired. The whole rest of the day was just more confusing and tiring.

The next day I was still tired but not so much that I fell asleep during Mathers's morning report. I had decided to look at the cup as half full and remember that now we only had three people left who could be our mole. However, the day had other plans in store for Hope and me. Half way through our searching of the Internet for information on Mathers and Nikhil (I had already checked Gray, so while he wasn't off the list he wasn't our focus), we were interrupted by Jasper.

"Guys, I'm really sorry about this but we need you right now. " He paused and seemed to fumble with words for a bit then continued. "We need people to go and try to find Alex and Claire. Ben and Harrison will give you directions to where they were last, but then after that you're on your own. Please, we really need your help. You guys have been into the ventilation system before so you have experience with that, and plus you guys did amazing on that teamwork test, and you're going to need a lot of teamwork to rescue them. So will you?" he asked hopefully, and in a pleading voice. We looked at each other. For once I couldn't tell what she was thinking. At the same time we both gave our answer.

"Yea--no." We looked at each other, both with looks of disbelief and questioning on our faces. This was the first time we had disagreed since our disagreement on whether to join the organization. I thought about that, and though I knew it had only been a few weeks since then, to me it felt like it had been year ago when we had been sitting in Mathers' office.

"One second," said Hope smiling at Jasper, then turned on me as Jasper walked away.

"We shouldn't do this. It could be and probably is a big trap, especially if the mole tells his friends over at the DFF.

Who knows what they might try to do- or do to us!" she said, pleading with me to side with her. I felt like I should side with her, and I knew that the old me would've sided with her, but I wasn't old me anymore.

"I know there are risks and there will most likely be DFF guards there waiting to capture us, but we have to try. As far as we know they might kill Alex and Claire if we don't get to them in time. Come on, Hope," I pleaded with her. She gave me a very mad look but then called Jasper back and told him we were in.

He practically jumped for joy when we told him this and seemed to be as happy as a little child given an ice cream cone. He ran back down to the meeting, though I'm sure he would have skipped if he had been alone. We followed him to the room at a slower pace and when we got in everyone seemed to have as much energy as Jasper, though a lot of them didn't seem as happy. As soon as we got in Ben launched into a full explanation of his new tactics.

"Okay, so because there are almost definitely people waiting for you there we have put a new system to help you. If there is any big trouble, just turn off your tracking devices briefly, and then turn them back on again as a signal. We will then send reinforcements to your location to help you out. Got it?" He talked very fast, but I still understood him. I nodded, and then Hope nodded too. He clapped his hands together and went to go get the equipment, I assumed. When he came back seconds later Mathers was there with him and I realized too late that he was going to tell Mathers about the operation.

He of course would tell the others who would go snitch on our mission to the DFF, if not Mathers himself doing that, though some part of me just didn't peg him as a mole. He had been shady and at first I thought he was slightly weird or crazy, but I had seen enough to prove both of those claims wrong. Still, I didn't think it was Gray; he had been so nice and encouraging; and from what we had seen of Nikhil he seemed like a pretty nice guy. None of them seemed like a mole. Though somehow the one I could really see being a traitor was Gray. I hated to think it, but if I had to choose, I definitely wouldn't have picked out Gray. I don't know what it was, but I could see him being a traitor to the DFF more than Mathers, or even Nikhil who I barely knew.

I pushed the mole out of my mind and looked down to see myself putting on my tracking device and pressing it once, so that it flashed green. I nodded, and looked back up to see Hope next to me with her tracker already on and ready to go. I turned back to where Ben, Harrison, and all the others were sitting. I waved to them, then without a backwards glance I turned and set out towards Alex and Claire.

Chapter Eighteen
The Rescue Mission

After a long wait at the monorail station, and a ride to the first ship we got ready to enter the oxygen ducts for a second time. I don't know if all the time spent just sitting around had affected me, but I was starting to rethink my decision to go with the mission.

The cowardice inside of me was fighting to regain power over my judgement, but I wouldn't let it. As I climbed up and into the small tunnel I fought a mental battle inside. Fear has a quite a sharp sword, but courage, if wielded correctly, can face anything. My body kept moving on auto-pilot until finally courage pushed fear back into its small corner on the edge of my brain. I turned off my mental auto pilot just in time to hear Harrison say,

"Okay turn left here and pop out the grate, then you'll be at their last known location. I would say to start from there and then go outward to the other rooms. Remember, this is DFF territory so there are going to be patrol. Try not to get caught."

We turned to face the grate and immediately as we began towards the grate I noticed a faint, yet distinct sound of people talking. I knew we were supposed to keep quiet so again I went through the slow process of dismantling the grate.

After a few painstaking minutes the grate popped off its hinges. I pushed it out slowly, then held on tightly as it almost fell. Grate in hand I clumsily pulled myself out of the duct, and fell hard on the wood floor. I got up and brushed off my clothes, hoping that nobody had heard. The talking was louder now and I could make out bits and pieces of a conversation.

"-Earth. Can you imagine how we would be without her?" said a deep male voice. I cautiously walked over to the wall and put my ear to it. I heard a slightly higher voice begin to talk.

"I know. Without her, they probably would have figured out our plan by now." I pulled my ear away from the wall, thinking. She? They seemed to be talking about the mole, but they had referred to it as a she, though there were no more women on our list. I couldn't figure it out but the thought was pushed from my mind when Hope tapped me on the shoulder.

"Time to go." She whispered. I nodded and followed her, both of us tiptoeing along, to the door. We stopped and she slowly pulled the door open, making a few creaks. Then as we tiptoed out the door, I noticed the talking. Well, I didn't really notice the talking, more the silence. Just a minute ago I could have sworn that there were two guards talking in the hallway, yet now they seemed to be non-existent. I realized my mistake too late.

Guards jumped out at us from both directions. Both of us were caught off guard, though while Hope got lucky and the attacker's blade missed, I wasn't as lucky. I turned my head just to see the guard, who had been hiding in the frame of one of the doors, slice a deep gash into my arm.

Pain exploded in my arm, then multiplied and infested my body. I cringed, but tried to keep my focus on dodging the attacks of the guard, which seemed to be getting harder each time. I clutched at my arm, which was spewing out blood at an alarming rate. I tried to focus on breathing relatively normally, but that was very hard when I was dodging a knife that could make my wound look like a minor scrape. With huge effort I managed to disarm the guard and then, instead of knocking him out, I had a different idea. I punched him as hard as I could, pushing him to the wall. I then pushed him to the ground, and put one leg on him to hold the guard there. I pulled my fist back as if to hit him, but instead I asked him a question in my most intimidating voice possible.

"Where are they?" I almost yelled.

"Whoa whoa man don't hurt me! They're in the room down this hallway, to the left and it will be the first on the right," he said, in a scared voice. I smiled, and let him go. I stood up to see Hope approaching me, with the unconscious body of the other guard behind her.

"To the left and then second on the right," I told her quickly and we set off towards where Alex and Claire were being hidden. We were speeding towards the room, and so when we turned I failed to see the man I had interrogated picking up his knife.

We soon got to the door and I signaled for Hope to stop. I leaned against the wall for support then clutched my hurt arm. It was still bleeding profusely, and hurting more by the second. I wiped the blood off, pulled myself together and kicked open the door.

I had already expected what I saw. There were five guards, no, five soldiers waiting for us there, and behind them were Alex and Claire, both bound to a chair and gagged. We took the soldiers by surprise and we gained a small advantage by this, but they already had the upper hand. They were positioned to get us in a way that blocked off the whole room and pushed us out. Also my throbbing arm made me sloppy and an easy target. Knowing that this battle had slim odds of us winning, I used my arm to turn my locater off and then on again in between a slice. Still dodging and weaving, I looked over at Hope, who was fighting three at once, unlike me with only two.

My distractions were what hurt me. Calling for reinforcements and looking at Hope had given one of my attackers enough time to aim a very good slice. I looked back to him and saw it just in time so that I was able to pull away, at least partially. I only got a small scrape on my right arm, which, though small still hurt almost as much as the other cut, and bled just the same. My pain was beginning to win the battle for my senses and my vision got blurry for a second. In that moment I realized how little our chances of winning the fight were. I tried not to think about this, and concentrated harder than ever on dodging. Then I gathered up all my remaining strength and got ready. For the millionth time one of the guards aimed his knife at me, but in a sudden burst of speed I grabbed it, and smashed the side of the blade against his head, knocking him out. I tried to hit the other guard, but he was ready for it and deflected my blow with his own blade. My adrenaline rush was fading fast and quickly I tried to use some advanced moves, using the knife as my second hand. He was able to block most of my attacks, except for one, which hit him hard. He fell back, and with a crash he hit the floor. Suddenly the thought of coming out of the battle with Alex and Claire was like a beacon of hope in my mind, pushing out the darkness. Using the time I had gotten from knocking down the man, I stole a glance at Hope. She was no longer fighting three, instead she finishing one man who was helpless, on the ground. I looked at her too long.

My legs were swept out from under me, and I looked up to see the guard smirking triumphantly above me. His beady eyes hovered on me for a second then looked up and widened. Hope was striding towards him with a knife in her hand. Even to me, she looked menacing. In two swift moves, she hit him across the head and then kicked him in the side. In that moment I saw a fire in Hope's eyes that I never seen before. The man crumpled to the ground, unconscious, and Hope held out a hand to me.

"Jordan!" She called my name out but my eyes were not on her. Instead they were fixed on a point way beyond her, on the guard that was approaching. I pointed, but it was already too late. The man slammed the side of his knife against her head and she crumpled, just as the guard she had taken out had. The man saw my open eyes and walked over to me next. He looked down at me and I recognized him. He was the guard I had interrogated for the whereabouts of Alex and Claire. Obviously letting him go hadn't been the brightest idea. He smiled, lifted his foot up to kick me and smashed it down with surprising force. I tried to hold onto my consciousness, but my efforts weren't enough. Within five seconds my world slid into blackness.

Chapter Nineteen
The Mole

I awoke in my own bed. I looked around to confirm what my senses were telling me, that it was my room. I looked to beside my bed and saw Katia, Ben and Kate, all sitting in chairs which had been pulled from my table. I sat up and memories broke back through whatever subconscious dam was holding them back. The fights came back, the mission and the end.

"What happened, where are--" I was cut short by Kate, who cleared her throat over my talking and then began.

"We were practically waiting for your reinforcement call. The reason no one else came was that nobody wanted to go. Everyone thought it was a trap, and no one was brave enough. We were lucky, because we caught the monorail just as it came, otherwise... I don't know. Anyway we got to you guys, and Hope wasn't there. Two men were picking up your unconscious body to take you... Somewhere, wherever they took Hope. We were able to get you, as well as Alex and Claire, because they were tied up in the room next to you. So in a way the mission was a success, though you are very beat up. You have two gashes on your arm, and countless bruises. It's going to hurt to do pretty much anything other than lie down, and hurt a lot to do actual work. You can stay home today."

I was stunned. I laid back down, but only to contemplate what Kate and just said. Alex and Claire were back, but Hope had been taken and now it could take weeks to find her, much more to get her back. How could I have let this happen to her, I thought. If I could have got up, or told her more quickly about the guard approaching her... Why, I thought, mad at myself. If just I had done either of those, Hope would be safe and the mission would have been completely successful. It was my fault. My fault. I drifted back into sleep, guilt pressing down on me.

I dreamed I was back in the hallway. Hope was reaching her hand out to pick me up, but I was looking at the man approaching. In a split second I remembered what was going to happen, and I tried to yell, but my mouth wasn't working. Then, though I wasn't moving it, my finger went out to point to the man but he was already there. I tried to get onto my feet as the man smashed Hope, but my body was super-glued into place on the floor. I was forced to watch for the second time as Hope crumpled to the ground, and I, helpless, wasn't long behind. Again I saw the foot being raised above me saw it hit, and felt the pain. Except this time the pain wasn't from the foot. It was from the loss of Hope, at my hands. The world went black once again, but this time I heard the voice of Hope crying out to me.

"Jordan!" I awoke with a start, covered in sweat. I was even shaking a little. I pulled myself out of my bed, and immediately saw why Kate and all of them hadn't wanted me working. My legs looked like a spatter painting: they were speckled with black, blue and purple bruises. I tentatively took steps, which were hard and hurt very much. Slowly and painfully I made my way into the kitchen where I saw my phone resting on the counter, like nothing had happened. I picked it up and looked at the date. I almost dropped the phone. It was the fourth of September. I had been asleep for at least two days. For a second I forgot that I was heavily bruised and walking caused me pain. I put down my phone, grabbed my jacket and went out the door of my quarters.

My forgetting of pain was short lived though, for as I approached the monorail the previous pain of walking came back, and this time it had doubled in size. I stopped and bent down, clutching my legs, which felt like the were exploding. I took deep breaths, in and out, trying to forget about the stabbing pain in my legs. I took one final deep breath then started to walk again, this time much, much slower than before. After more slow walking, which was becoming less painful by the step, I got to the monorail. It seemed like it had been waiting for me all the time I had been unconscious.

The monorail ride was crowded, and at first I was confused before remembering it was lunch time. I looked down at my stomach, realizing that I hadn't eaten in at least two days. Also since no one at work would be exactly expecting me, I could take a break. It was then that I noticed the sound. It wasn't exactly creaking, more of a scraping sound. I frowned, for the monorail had been as smooth as jello as long as I could remember. It was like... I couldn't think of what could be wrong. Then the sound stopped and the monorail went on sounding like it always did, smooth and perfect. I was very much intrigued by this, but my thoughts were cut short by the station coming into view. As it did the thought of lunch resurfaced in my head, and my stomach grumbled in response.

I decided that because I was hurt and feeling sorry for myself, I would treat myself to a very fancy lunch: a footlong sub and milkshake at Sandwich Way. I usually didn't eat at Sandwich Way because their sandwiches didn't cost much as their milkshakes did, and I knew if I went there I would come back with a milkshake. In a minute I was sitting at a table with a sub in one hand and a milkshake in the other hand. It was the perfect lunch for my beaten up self.

Afterwards I went back up Asia street then to America street. Walking was getting easier, and the pain involved was at a minimal for the day. I got into our offices and saw no one, then remembered that they were probably out for lunch. I sat down at our old desk, and looked straight ahead without seeing anything. All that rang through head was: 'your fault'. It echoed and echoed and I didn't know how to stop it. Luckily a distraction arrived in form of all the other teams. They were all chattering as usual and when Katia, who was at the beginning of the group, exclaimed:

"Look who it is! He's back!" She came running and gave me a hug which I returned. Everyone followed her and came in a semi-circle around me.

"Hey everybody!" I said in a cheerful tone, trying to fake a happy smile, and by the reflected smiles back from everyone I assumed it looked like I was just as happy as I wanted to be.

I wanted to be happy to see them, I wanted to be happy that I was back, but there was always a part of my mind listening to the echoes of 'your fault'. The semi-circle dissipated and I sat back down at my desk looking for something, anything to distract myself. I looked around and saw the forgotten suspect list. It would be the perfect distraction, I thought, and it would help out everyone else. I thought about what to start with, seeing as I only had three suspects left. I had almost finished all the questions for an interview when a voice aroused me out of my work.

"Jordan? Umm, I think I might have something that could help with your search." I looked up. It was Claire. I blinked and then replied.

"Okay, then. What is it?" I asked in reply and she hesitated then began again.

"Well, I was captured, as you very well know, and while tied up I did manage to catch some information on the mole from the guards. They thought we were out of earshot but I actually could hear their conversation. They didn't actually reveal who the mole was... But they always referred to him as a he. Anyway I hope that helps!" she said, and left to go back into the meeting room. I sighed. A few days ago that would have helped, but now, it didn't do anything other than clearly prove that it couldn't be the woman at the front desk, I thought. I leaned back. I had really hoped that she was going to tell me who the mole really was, but she hadn't. The mole was a man, the one piece of information that couldn't help. If they had said it was a girl, then-- wait a minute, I almost shouted out loud. I had just remembered two things.

First of all, Alex and Claire were still suspects, since they had been with the DFF when we had done the test to see if the mole was on any of the teams. Second, I had heard the guards talking about the mole as a she when they *definitely* didn't know anybody was listening. This could mean two things. First, it could mean that Claire was the mole and was trying to get me off her trail. Second, it could mean that the woman at the front desk actually was the mole. Either way, the mole wasn't who we thought. Quickly, I formed a plan and strode into the meeting room, where Claire was looking as innocent as ever, crouching next to Harrison saying something. I walked to the front of the room, where Mathers stood every morning. After all, the announcement I was about to make was more important than Mathers' morning recap most days. I cleared my throat very loudly and all the people in the room looked to me, and I noticed that Mathers was sitting right there, as if waiting for me. All the better, I thought. The bigger audience the better.

"Hello everybody. Umm, for a while now we have known that someone in our very ranks is secretly working for the DFF. As long as we've known that, my partner and I have been working tirelessly to find out who this 'mole' is. Finally, today, I have big news on that. With the help of Claire, I have figured out who the mole is. Could you please come up here Claire. After all it was your information that made me find this traitor." I smiled at her, showing no signs that I was about to call her out as a mole. I figured that it was a 50/50 chance, and I couldn't forget the woman at the front desk did seem to hate her husband a lot. Claire reached me and I continued.

"Using Claire's information I have eliminated everybody except for one person. The mole is Claire! She revealed herself to me by trying to make sure she wasn't a suspect, didn't you Claire?" I said, smiling at Claire, who looked surprised and disbelieving. Then her whole face changed into a face of malice. I expected her to run, but she didn't. Instead she did something much worse. She pulled out a object from her jacket that I had only seen in pictures.

"Recognize this?" She said, in a voice completely different from her normal high voice, as she pointed a gun to my head.

Chapter Twenty
Failed

I froze. The gun might be a prototype and not work, I thought hopefully in my head, but that wouldn't be a chance worth taking.

"If any of you move, Jordan dies." she grabbed me and started pulling me towards the door.

"All of you have messed up big time. You say violence isn't the answer but then you use it against the DFF. Don't you see? You're fighting for the wrong side. Violence is the only way to win. This organization you have won't stop us, and our plan for you. The DFF shall rule!" And with that, she let me go, then turned and ran out the door of the meeting room, then out of the whole building.

The room erupted into chaos. Everyone was trying to get out, or yell something, or go after Claire. I opened the door again, and everyone save for a couple went out. I was one of the three to run to the door of the place. I needed to catch

Claire. If I could catch her, I could find Hope, and if I could find Hope then everything would be good again. Sort of. I ran down America street faster than I ever had before and soon I was far ahead of all the others who were running.

Then the pain came back. I had completely forgotten that I still was the human splatter painting and I couldn't run. I stopped to get myself together again as my legs were transformed into a harbor of excruciating ships of pain. My hands formed into fists and I fought to cry out in pain. You have to get up, I told myself and slowly, shakily, I did. I started to walk slowly, then I got up to normal speed. Still, it didn't even close to match how fast the people running by me were. I knew that unless I got very, very lucky then I wouldn't catch Claire.

Some very long minutes later, I stood at the monorail station where all the others were, waiting for me. Claire had gotten away. I sat down. If I hadn't been so hurt I was almost sure I could have caught Claire. Then again, I thought to myself, if I hadn't been hurt then I may have beaten my attackers fast enough to save Hope. All my injuries had brought was failure, from my point of view. I looked down at my arm which was beginning to heal, and then my many bruises which seemed to be losing their luster.

"Don't blame this on yourself, Jordan." I looked up. It was Katia.

"It's not your fault that you're hurt," she said, in a nice voice. I nodded, not saying anything. "Look I'm sorry, and I know you think it's your fault that Hope-" she stopped after seeing the look in my eyes at the mention of her name. She knew she had gone too far. "I... I'm sorry," she stuttered, then walked away, back out of the Monorail station.

As my muscles began to calm down, I sat down on a bench and a wave of fatigue hit me like a sac of boulders. I slowly stood back up, and decided that I wouldn't be missed, and Katia would understand, at least somewhat. I stretched and as I did the monorail pulled into station, ready to take me home. I stepped through its doors, with the boulders of fatigue and the iron bars of guilt pushing me down, an ever-present reminder of failure. I sat down and watched the station speed away and get replaced by the vastness of space.

Then suddenly the noise was back. It was a definitely a scraping noise, I thought. But what could the monorail be scraping against, I asked myself. The only remotely possible way the noise could've started was if someone placed something under or around the monorail, but why would anyone do that? Then just as quickly as it had started the noise was gone. The questions filled my head, so I decided not to think about the noise and its origin. Instead, a different question surfaced in my head. When was N.E.S.S. getting to Earth? I asked myself. Time was still a jumble for me, because I had been out for so long. I got out my phone to search when we were expected to arrive at the solar system; if the solar system was still there, then Earth would be. Then I remembered that I couldn't get Internet while on the monorail.

When the monorail finally came to a stop, and I had hobbled back to my quarters, I got back to my search. It turned out there was a whole website devoted to counting down to when we would reach the solar system, and then the Earth. The clock for the solar system read: 3d: 2h 45m 34s. I watched slowly as the seconds went down to 30 to 25 then I snapped out of it and scrolled down the page. As well as the two countdowns, the page had an article explaining different things about the countdowns, which I read. The article told me that once we actually got to the solar system (if Earth was still there) we would have to slow down, find Earth then travel to it at a slow cruising speed. In other words, this just added another 2 and a half hours or so to the countdown. I looked over to the Earth countdown and saw that this was right, it had 3d 5h 13m 5s left. I turned off my phone, put it in my pocket, and went to lay down. I was still very fatigued. I looked at the time on my phone to see that it was 2:04 P.M.. The truth would be revealed at 4:30 in 3 days, I thought to myself, and then more than a month of waiting could finally pay off. We could finally see Earth once more. The DFF would have failed.

Chapter Twenty-One
The Final Prep

For the next two days, I was bedridden. After getting beat up on the mission with Hope, having a gun pointed at my head, and chasing Claire, I had been tired and sore.

When I got up, I was still slightly sore, but I felt nothing I had been feeling for the two days before. I stretched, then tried jogging in place, and to my surprise it felt quite nice to run again. I got dressed, scarfed down some breakfast, grabbed my things, and was out.

After sitting in bed doing nothing for two days, the whole ship seemed to be teeming with energy. I got on the monorail, and within minutes I was back where I belonged, at #46 America street. I went back through the old hallway and for the second time in three days, was greeted with smiles and a general welcome. However the smiles vanished quickly as everyone gathered in the meeting room. The seat where

Claire had sat was empty, and a dark silence surrounded it. After a lifetime, Mathers broke the cold silence.

"Welcome back, Jordan. Another two days have gone by, and today we should be finally ready. Ready to take down the DFF. To catch you up, Jordan, we've found that the DFF center of operations is actually in the basement of the first ship, a secret storage place that was not on any blueprints, thus making it the perfect hideout for the DFF. For the last day and a half, ever since we found this out we have been forming a plan that will come into motion today. Also, we finally got new earpieces so you can relay back information to us. Now, we have work to do, let's get to it." He finished and walked out of the room, bringing all the silence out with him. The teams began grouping and talking to each other, and as they did, Harrison came over to me.

"So, the plan goes like this." He pulled up a 3-D model of the first ship, which now had a new floor that was represented in green. "So, judging by our our model, which we made using the pictures from when Katia found it, the main entrance is a corrupt-looking maintenance hatch which leads down to their lair. There are guards guarding that entrance, but we're sure nobody is guarding the vents. Right now we have the element of surprise to help us, so we need them to think everything is going right until there's no way not to be seen..." He continued telling me the plan, and when he finished, it brought a smile to my face. We were going to take down the DFF.

Chapter Twenty-Two
Plans in Motion

Half an hour later, I was standing at the monorail station of the first ship with every team left except for Ben and Harrison, who were back at base watching over us through the holograms, and Jasper and Skyler, who had gone ahead to clear the entrance for us.

We walked down the hallways in silence, all anticipating what was to come. After three turns, we made it to the entrance. Jutting out from the wall, it looked just as Harrison had described it, like a forgotten maintenance hatch with no meaning. The hatch might once have been shiny, but the years had taken their toll; It was dull and plated with rust. As I gripped the handle, paint chips came off, then slowly, the hatch opened. Inside lay a dark vertical passageway, which had a ladder leading down into the depths of the basement.

"Ladies first," I said, gesturing to the ladder. Kate sighed, and pulled herself through the hatch. As she began down, the ladder smacked against the passageway, making a loud clank each time she went down a rung. Clank, clank, clank, went the ladder as two others began down. The ladder kept clanking as I pulled myself onto it. Slowly I climbed down the dank passageway, and over the clanking, I heard Kate's cry of "all clear" meaning that the entrance guards had been forcibly switched out for Jasper and Skyler wearing phony DFF suits. They would continue to guard the entrance for us so that if anything went wrong we wouldn't have much trouble getting out.

After a minute, and more clanking though it was muffled, everybody was down the ladder and ready to move on. We stood on the edge of a long hallway, with doorways and turns everywhere. Now comes the tricky part, I thought.

We didn't know exactly where the center of the hideout was because of our limited knowledge of the place, and for that reason, we had to split up. When we came to the first split in the hallway, a three-way split, we broke into teams. Alex and I grouped, since both of our partners were gone, and the rest grouped normally. We chose the middle path, and continued on without the others. With only one other person there, the basement seemed very eery, though it was brightly lit.

Suddenly we heard movement from farther up the hall. It looked perfectly straightforward, but there must have been a branch, because as we froze, a man in DFF attire walked out from the left and went straight down what must have been the right branch.

"Follow." I said in a barely audible whisper, and gestured diagonally towards where the man was. We crept along the hallway, not making a sound. When we reached the split I checked quickly for anyone around the corner, then we began to follow the man at a good distance. Soon he turned another corner and we had to speed-walk to catch up with him. We stopped at the corner, but the man came back out.

"Don't think I couldn't hear you," the man said with malice, and took us by surprise with a blow to my legs. I fell to the ground, and Alex seemed to be frozen as the man swept his legs off the ground.

"If you thought you could come in here unnoticed, then you really have screwed up," he said, and as he did, three other heavily armed guards appeared around us. We were dead.

I quickly looked around, trying to see if there was any exit that we could run to. There wasn't. We had run right into a trap. My mind was on overdrive, and adrenaline was pumping through my veins after being hit. I racked my brains for some way I could get out. I couldn't think of a way, so I decided it was best to go down fighting. I jumped up, and to their surprise, I pushed two of the armored guards away and kicked down the other. Alex got up too, but before I could knock out the man who we had been trailing, the guards got back up.

"I'll hold them off," said Alex, as the first guard threw a punch at him. I nodded and turned back to the DFF official, who took a gun out of its holster. Instincts took over, and I hit the gun out of his hand into mine.

"Where is the control center, and where are you hiding Hope?" I yelled, stuffing as much malice into my voice as possible. I knew I'd never shoot this man, but I was hoping he wouldn't call my bluff. The man looked flustered and scared, then he cracked.

"Straight on from here, then second right, then left." he said, slowly putting his hands up. I smiled then, remembered the last time. I hit the man's head with the butt of the gun and he went limp.

Turning back around I watched, frozen for a second, as Alex was overpowered. The three guards were killing him and I was frozen. Then my body came to. I jumped into the fight, and briefly had the element of surprise. I kicked one of them in the face, and caught by surprise, his knees buckled. Looking down at him, I saw that a sword was sheathed at his side and I pulled it out. I smacked him with the hilt, then brandished it at the other two. They flinched and jumped away from Alex.

I raised the blade as if to swing at them, but instead I swiftly kicked their feet out from under them, knocking them to the ground. Then, before they could get up I smashed their heads together with the hilt.

"Straight on from here, then second right, then left. Let's go." I motioned in the direction of place, then took off with Alex at my heels. We ran straight and I began to feel more of the mounting pressure. I suddenly realized that the man could have just as easily lied as told the truth. I suddenly realized we could be running into a huge trap. There was no time for thought, though. Trap or not, it was our only chance at finding Hope, and shutting down the DFF once and for all.

We turned at the second right and found ourselves at a plain wooden office door with no special markings or plaque to signify its importance, I thought to myself, unless it really had no importance. I kicked open the door, and to my relief the head of the DFF stood there, with the huge server behind him and Hope tied up on the side.

I realized too late he was pointing a gun straight at us as he shot Alex.

Chapter Twenty-Three
Ray Blackworth

Alex seemed to fall in slow motion, a look of utter surprise on his face as the light sped out of his eyes and he fell into death. I had no time for grieving though, because as I watched, Ray Blackworth began to reload. I thought of all my rage towards him, for kidnapping Hope, for killing Alex, for leading the DFF, and I focused it into one kick.

Wham! His head was smacked up by my kick, and in surprise he dropped the gun. I picked it up, and masked my face with rage, just as I had done to the other guard.

"Give up now!" I yelled with my most intimidating voice. The man laughed, and put his hands up. I started to inch forward but as I did he smacked his hands down onto the server, pressing three different buttons. All of a sudden the screen lit up with a big timer counting down from two and a half minutes.

"No. You give up. In two and a half minutes the monorail will blow up, severing the connection between this ship and the others. If Earth is truly here then we'll crash into it, dying and causing massive destruction on Earth. On the other hand, depending on the time, you never know. We might just get lucky enough to have the monorail reach the middle ship and blow N.E.S.S. into three separate ships, all sentenced to death. Now surrender or die!"

This time I was dumbfounded, and taking this to his advantage, Ray smacked the gun out of my hand. He punched me in the nose and I felt blood rushing out, but I also felt the rush of adrenaline. He threw another punch, but I caught it and twisted his arm around and kicked him in the chest. He cried out in pain but kept his guard up. I tried many more kicks and punches but he blocked all of them, then slid behind me. I was taken by surprise and Ray pulled my arms behind my back and held. He then spoke again.

"Give up now. There are more coming. The monorail is going to blow and we'll escape using the old pods. Give up!" He yelled menacingly.

"Never. The DFF will end here and now." I retorted and kicked him backwards and the blood in my ears began to pump a symphony to our fight. I hit him again and again, taking out all the anger I had on the DFF. Finally as he stumbled backwards I hit him across the face with one arm, and hit up with the other. Plus one for Jordan, I thought to myself as Ray fell to the ground.

Quick as the monorail I looked back at the countdown, but was relieved to see I had a minute left. I pulled out my phone and went immediately to my calculator which then turned into my hacking device. I scanned the local wifi for devices and easily found the server. The password was easy to bypass but then I came upon a dilemma as my phone accessed the server. I still should have been able to control it, but the phone had gone blank. It was like the computer had nothing on it, and definitely wasn't hosting a giant encrypted server.

Then I realized what the computer was. It was an illegal type of computer which held two sides, one that could be easily accessed and one that was completely hidden under the first, and triple-encrypted. If anyone (like me) tried to hack it it would show the public side and there would be no way to get to the other. These types were banned after many criminals walked free because the incriminating evidence was on the hidden side.

The time was ticking and I didn't know how to stop the bombs from being detonated. So I tried my only other option. Closing my eyes I kicked through the computer's screen. Giant pieces of glass and wire embedded themselves into my foot as kicked it but I didn't stop. I opened my eyes when I was content it was broken. Then, for good measure, I used the knife at Ray's feet to slice through the cords connecting the computer to wherever the power source was. I had stopped the bombs, or so I thought.

"No! No! No, please no! Don't! That will ruin it all. I don't want it to go! Please stop!" I looked back and saw Ray with eyes wide, full of fear. I didn't understand how he had seemed so confident yet now was pleading.

"It's done, Ray. It's over," I said, and I see could him grow even more sad. I even saw a glistening tear roll down his cheek as he mouthed the word 'NO'.

Suddenly, I felt an explosion hurl me into the air. It wasn't lethal, but it made my already broken leg even worse. I looked at Ray's body, which was blown to bits. One last bomb had been planted inside of him, just in case the others failed. I felt a brief pang of regret.

Next, I turned and limped over to Hope, who was still bound and gagged. Using the same knife, I cut her free. She gave me a swift crushing hug, then slapped me.

"Where have you been?" she yelled with surprising anger.

"Trying to save N.E.S.S., if you couldn't see. I'm sorry it took so long but what the heck? Did you really have to have to hit me? Haven't I been through enough?" I asked. The pain in my foot was really getting to me. Hope put her hands on her hips, but remained silent.

"Come on now, we have to get out of here before anyone else gets here, and that won't be long," I said, gesturing out. Hope nodded and followed as we jogged silently down the hall.

Six minutes later, we were back at the entrance, and I had filled Hope in on what had happened since her kidnapping. When we got to the entrance, Jasper and Skyler were still posted there and they followed us out, meaning that everyone else had already came back. I told them of our battles and how Alex died from Ray Blackworth. It was all over now, I thought. This was it.

Epilogue
One Day Later

I had gotten back the day before and had brought cheers of thanks but also mourning for Alex's death. Earth was there. The solar system was just how we had left it. As we came closer to landing time I marveled at The planet out the window. The ship was saved.

By lunch of the next day we had entered the solar system. It was beautiful. Finally seeing the sun and all the planets was breathtaking. The great blue of Neptune, and the hues of Jupiter were amazing.

Landing was a hassle. Everyone was eager to get off, and so a big commotion started at the landing bay in the third ship. The monorail was crowded, the first ship was crowded with people packing, and of course so was the third ship. I stood near a window, quite far back from the actual doors, but still with a good view. I watched as the green plains of Earth grew closer and closer. Then the plain green divided into different shades, which were in little squares. Finally I closed my eyes and felt the jolt which I had been waiting for.

We were on Earth. The landing doors opened and the sunlight almost blinded me. I got used to it quickly, though, I saw the green paradise of Earth spread out in front of us. After a little struggling I was able to step off the ship. I laid down on the grassy plain and looked up at the great blue sky and the sun. I looked to my right and saw the outline of a city in the distance. It was time for a new start, a new beginning, a new Earth.

www.ingramcontent.com/pod-product-compliance
Ingram Content Group UK Ltd.
Pitfield, Milton Keynes, MK11 3LW, UK
UKHW041943190726
13854UKWH00004B/1760